craving submission
PLAYERS AND SINNERS

NANCY CHASTAIN

www.authornancychastain.com

Developmental Editor: Dr. Plot Twist. *More information available @ www.drplottwist.com*

Cover Design: Touch Creations Designs

Series Organization: Rewritten Fairytales

Craving Submission is dedicated to all individuals that know who they are sexually and aren't afraid to express their desires.

Also, to the survivors of less-than-perfect childhoods. Despite these beginnings, they are determined to do whatever needed to accomplish their dreams.

Be yourself and chase your dreams, don't let anyone or anything stop you.

I believe in you.

lust

What is *Lust*?

Lust has several meanings. You can lust after money. People can lust after power, but... hearing the word lust, most people's mind goes to sex. Lust is that insatiable sexual desire and the craving for gratification that comes with it.

prologue

SABLE

"To be a good Dom, you must first know the power the submissive holds," Ms. Sally says as she points to the sex toys on the wall, some of which look more like torture devices than anything capable of causing pleasure. "But you don't have to worry about any of this, Sable."

"So..." I clear my throat and take a moment to gather my thoughts. Worrying is something I've been doing since I learned to walk. It's not that easy to just turn off the little red flags that pop up out of nowhere. "You said you had a job for me?"

Ms. Sally smiles softly and shuts the door to the playroom. "Yes," she confirms and points in the opposite direction of the exit. "It's right down the hall."

I have no fucking clue what I had gotten myself

into, but the dark hallway in front of us seems a lot less scary than the alley I had been sleeping in, so I follow her deeper into this den, every once in a while, glancing behind me to keep the exit within sight.

"Are you going to tell me what it is?" Just because she had saved me from getting arrested for shoplifting some food, doesn't mean... Well, I don't really know what it means. I just know seventeen and homeless by no means entails stupidity.

"Ms. Sally, since you know, we're in here and I'm grateful for all your help, but I... I just want to make it very clear..." I stop along with her and stand up straight —adamant about my position. "If I wanted guys to ogle me and try to use me, I would have stayed at my Mama's house."

At least here I'd get paid. The thought creeps up my spine as I settle the little quiver in my throat.

Ms. Sally shifts back in shock and then studies me for a little too long. Her hand lingers near the doorknob as if she contemplates whether or not to send me on my way.

I swallow as it turns.

"Sable, although I'm concerned about what you said, you don't have the experience to be one of my regulars... I had a little something different in mind."

The door swings open to a closet full of cleaning

products. A few mops hang on the backside, next to a broom.

"Maybe you could help me keep this place clean?" She runs a finger along the broomstick. "My employees clean up after themselves, but in our off hours, I'd like to do a more thorough cleanse of the place."

"Oh." I glance around the hall.

"We pay cash, and I can offer you a room, a place to shower, and keep you safe, be that from the streets or from your homelife."

My heart swells as the tears accumulate in the corners of my eyes. "Thank you."

"But to accept, there's one condition.... Tell me about what happened at home."

This woman, who I didn't know from Adam, caught me, saved me, and trusted me all in a matter of hours.

The woman who gave birth to me—created me— did the exact opposite: doubted me, hurt me, then let me go. Though, I'm not sure the last part is all too bad. Seventeen and homeless was a lot safer than where I had grown up.

Ms. Sally rests a hand on her hip and with a loud sigh shakes her head. "Well, you don't have to tell me just yet. At least not until you're ready."

I glance behind her at the cleaning supplies, then down the length of the hallway, and flick my gaze over

the red letters above the door. There's nothing out there waiting for me, except the cold.

"My mother threw me out when I told her about one of the men making a pass at me," I blurt out rapidly.

Ms. Sally purses her lips but gently nods her head for me to continue.

"She accused me of leading him on and trying to steal him from her. Things got... *ugly*... and I had just enough time to fill my backpack with some clothes."

"I see. How long have you been away from home?" she closes the door gently and leans against it.

"One week. And I'm never going back." I glance at Ms. Sally and, in case she doubted my conviction, I straightened my spine and reiterated the last part, "Never."

I shake my head as the image of my screaming mom pops into my head. I'll never forget the way she made me feel like nothing. The way she looked through me. The way she didn't even watch me leave or bother to search for me. She threw me away like a crumpled hamburger wrapper. It took me far too long to scrape my heart up off the cement, and when I did, I was starving.

"Why is that?" she asks, curling her fingers around her upper arm and tapping her fingernails against the fabric of her blazer.

"Because no one's ever going to have the ability to make me cave ever again."

She smooths the material over her stomach and inches away from the wall, closer to me. As if she had a secret only, I could hear despite us being completely alone. "The power isn't what was wrong, Sable. The way it was used is what was wrong."

"Your current champion, Matt Jacobs, defends his title of MMA USA Heavy Weight Champion. He has an unmatched record of twenty-five wins by submission throughout the span of his career. No other fighter comes close to his record."

To get into my fighting mindset, I tune out the rest of the announcement regarding the other fighter and find my focus. The fans cheer me on, buzzing on the way I win. As I step forward, I can't help but wonder what they'd think if they knew just how far my need for submission went, in and out of the ring.

In my twenties, sex came with rules. Specifics. I'd tell her what I wanted and how I wanted her to be. Most of the women I had dated didn't like it. They said I was too aggressive or demanding.

But when I was twenty-five, I met an older woman

in her mid-thirties. She had a fantasy of being dominated. At the time, I had only heard the word dominate before, but she spurred my curiosity.

So, I researched, found a couple of underground clubs, and went to them. At first, I watched the scenes, studying other dominates to see the power dynamic. The relief and fluidity.

After striking up conversations with a few of the men I realized brute force and demanding were not the way to go. Simply requesting and mutual respect is what I was missing.

This is a revelation to me. While I'm in the ring I'm being forceful and controlling the situation by any means possible. I had to experience the differences to completely understand it was not something that came easy for me to learn, I had to find a gentler side of myself that I never knew existed.

I'll never get tired of standing in the middle of the ring and hearing the crowd's roar as my arm is raised in victory.

The announcer says, "Matt Jones, you are a two-time MMA USA Heavy Weight Champion." The flashes of the cameras are blinding.

After that, I'm pulled in several directions, everyone wanting their picture taken with me. Several minutes later, I put my arm around my manager's shoulder and lean in to tell him, "Get me the hell out of here, Eddie. I'm ready to party and get laid."

Eddie Langley inconspicuously answers, "You have to take pics with the sponsors, man. They were pissed last time when you disappeared. Give it another hour, and I'll get you out of here. Remember, they pay you a ton of money."

"One hour," I tell him, then plaster a fake smile on my face and saunter up to some men in suits. I have no clue who they are, but I have my photo taken with them anyway.

As the hour winds down, I finish the last photos with the ring girls, who are all employees of a local strip club. I invite them all to continue to party with us at the Dragon's Lair, a hot nightclub on Hollywood Boulevard. The owner is a friend, and the free publicity of me showing up after my fights when I'm in town helps both of us.

I'm climbing out of the ring when a woman in tight black jeans, a red blouse, and black hair, which hangs loosely down her back, catches my eye. Inviting her to celebrate with me quickly turns into my next submission project, not that I'm accustomed to hearing the word no from a woman.

As I step out of the ring, she tilts over one of the white wooden chairs. Her heart-shaped ass is perked up and in an optimal spanking position. She searches for something in her large purse; soft strands of her hair fall over her shoulder, exposing the delicate cure of her neck.

Kissable.

I pry my eyes off of her to check the floor for my in with her. Not that I've ever needed one before. But I find nothing on the floor but foiled confetti and left-over cups and bottles. When I glance up, she had turned to the side, allowing the light to hit the red, not-so-sheer material of her blouse, exposing a truth about her. She matches her bra to her shirt.

Now, that's hot.

I approach her with a craving I haven't felt for a woman. I can't put my finger on what it is about her, I just know I have a need to know her.

Her back is turned to me as I walk up to her, realizing she is almost six feet tall with her heels on.

I reach out to tap her on the shoulder. When she turns around, I peer into the most prominent black pupils I have ever seen. Her olive complexion is flawless. Her lips are perfectly pouted, making me want to grab and kiss her immediately.

She looks at me, surprised, then takes a deep breath. "Matt Jones, how does it feel to be the MMA USA Heavy Weight Champion for the second time by the opponent tapping?" She sticks a microphone in my face.

The term is submission, I think to myself while utterly annoyed that my dick waltzed me right into a trap.

"Fuck!" I say out loud.

Another damn reporter. Another someone trying to make a quick buck off *my* hard work. *No way.* Reporters twist everything and anything to get a hook, and I'm not going to get burned... again. I learned my lesson a long time ago: don't trust someone who sells headlines.

"What was that?" She guides the microphone to her mouth, drawing my attention to the glossy red lipstick coated on her plump lips. A tactic. A lure. Shiny things come with sharp edges. "Did you say something?"

"Great, it feels great," I stammer as I make my escape. No matter how insanely hot they are, reporters see successful athletes as meal tickets. I guarantee if I seduce her with the promise of an interview, she'd drop those jeans and show me that perfect heart-shaped ass.

A gentle squeeze against my shoulder stops me dead in my tracks. It's not just the touch... but the spark it sends down my spine and splays out across my ass cheeks renders me still. Like two swats to the rear. *Pow. Pow.*

Sore muscles, no doubt, in desperate need of some ice and rest, but I don't like it.

Not.

One.

Bit.

"What's next for you, Matt?"

"A hot shower," I respond, shrug her hand off my arm, and walk off.

The pale gray locker room calms me with its emptiness. The room holds nothing but benches to sit on, lockers, equipment, and doors to the showers. In here, the outside doesn't matter. Everything I had—every ounce of fight — I left out in the ring. Here, I can unwind away from the public eye and ground myself.

Before I can even take a seat, my manager shows up. Eddie props himself up against my locker with a don't-bullshit-me expression plastered on his face. Since we were kids, he's had that same damn look, just now there's a shit-ton more hair on his face then when we were ten.

"I got stopped by a rookie reporter." Sitting on the bench, I flip my wrists, baring the laces for Eddie to untie.

Eddie reaches in for my water bottle and places it beside me. "What, where?" He removes my gloves from my hands and hangs them up on the hook.

"Right outside the door," I answer and down half the bottle.

"I vet all the press invites after that last chick." Eddie shakes his head and goes silent while he stares at the locker room entrance. Those smarts of his probably have him running down a mental list of names. "You sure?"

I snort, then finish my water. "Pretty fuckin' sure."

Eddie has always had his shit together. While I devoted my time to making a name for myself in MMA, Eddie went to college and got a Bachelor of Science in sports management. He had always told me he was going to be my manager. I wasn't surprised when he made it happen. That's who he was and is now—he makes shit happen— and who can I trust more with my career than my best friend?

"I know all the press out there, and there wasn't a rookie," he concludes.

"She sure as hell had a mic and used it to ask me dumb questions like a rookie. I don't want to deal with that shit."

"Chill out. Take your shower so we can get to the club. You'll feel better when you have a couple of drinks and see all that ass begging to go home with you."

"I have a lot of energy to burn off. You better make sure I have some seasoned options tonight."

"I have called in a couple of pros to ensure you get what you need if you don't find it with the amateurs. I got you covered, man," Eddie assures me. He takes his phone out of his pocket as it rings. "I have to get this. "It's business." He walks out the door.

I undress and step under the hot, steaming water.

My dick is semi-hard from the adrenaline of the win. I made my opponent submit. It's the best way to win a fight, to unwind, and find my release.

I don't care if it's a fighter in the ring or a woman on her knees, I crave submission. There is nothing like having a trained, physically fit two-hundred-sixty-five-pound man tapping out and admitting defeat because I have the power over him. It's exhilarating, but nowhere near as freeing as a woman submitting to me—trusting me at her most vulnerable and allowing me to take her senses and her body to the brink of ecstasy. That is the most incredible turn-on.

I finish in the shower and wrap a towel around my waist, covering my now fully hard dick. Abstaining before a big fight has its downsides, but now that I've won, a celebration is in order. In anticipation of the evening ahead, I'm hyped up and ready for the night. I head back into the locker room to get dressed.

There, sitting on the bench, is the damn beautiful rookie from earlier.

"Get the fuck out!" I shout, dropping my towel. My nudity doesn't seem to faze her in the slightest. Her eyes go to my dick; her tongue sneaks out, wetting her bottom lip. My dick betrays me and jerks to life.

She takes a deep breath before speaking, "Listen, I get that you don't want to answer any of my questions but give me a minute." She stands, taking a step closer to me, her hand reaches out and runs her fingers across the worn leather of my gloves, hanging on the hook. "I'm trying to get my break to be a Sports reporter. If you give me a few minutes, it will help me out." She steps around me, handing me my jeans out of the open locker. "What do you say? Will you help me by giving me an interview?" Sable pleads her case, never taking her eyes off me as she sits back down on the bench. She nervously picks up my damp towel and folds it, before placing it on the bench

Jerking my jeans out of her hand, I pull them up my legs, then walk up to her. "Quid pro quo." This time I won't be the one who gets screwed over.

"What?" she asks, taking a seat.

"You heard me." I fasten my jeans and zip up, which isn't easy with my semi-hardon "Let's say, I do the interview and help you out, what's in it for me?" Looking at her directly, I step even closer—so close her next words could echo in my belly button. "If you get your big break, that means you'll owe me..."

She peeks up at me through her thick lashes, those soft doe eyes rounding with curiosity as she focuses on my every move. "What do you want?" she whispers softly.

I reach out, moving a hair off her cherub cheek. "What will you give me?"

That touch, in milliseconds, spurs a transformation

within her. Her body angles back, her head cocks to the side, and there's a smirk planted on the corner of her lips. Her fingers run between the crevices of the bench as she stretches out the one word: "Depends."

I'm not sure what it is about her, but I step forward. My knees are centimeters from the gray bench; my stance wide. Her legs are parted, sandwiching mine, which she doesn't seem to mind.

"I have a very vivid imagination, with particular wants..." I add. "I'm not sure your up to fulfilling them."

She smiles and motions to stand up. Without even realizing it, I shift back to give her room.

What the fuck?

We both realize what I had done at the same time. Without even trying, she commanded the room, the space, the distance between us. I'm both impressed and annoyed by it.

"Let's just say I don't gamble when something matters to me." She stands easily, then leans into me, sending shivers down my chest with her proximity to my neck. She whispers, "And the question isn't whether I can meet those needs, Matt. But rather if you can fulfill mine." She steps back and slides her purse over her shoulder. "I'm inclined to say you can't."

I hear the door to the locker room open. "Come on, man, you ready?" Eddie asks as he comes in. "Who do we have here?" He smiles and walks up to the reporter.

"This little one is the rookie reporter I told you about earlier. She is just about to tell me what she would give me if I gave her an interview." I cross my arms over my chest and turn back toward the reporter.

"Out you go, sweetheart. Matt doesn't have time for you this evening." Eddie grabs her by her arm and pulls her toward the door. Once she's outside, he says, "Persistent and beautiful little thing, isn't she? Those two combinations plus being a reporter is not something you need to get involved with. That can go wrong in so many ways." He pats me on the shoulder. "Let's go find someone to play with for the evening."

We go out the back door of the stadium into the waiting limo. The driver opens the door, and I'm greeted by two lovely ladies dressed for a night of sin. They slide apart, making room for me to nestle between them.

The first bottle of the night is popped.

two

SABLE

Matt is the type of man I would love to have on his knees in my dungeon.

Submitting to me.

Carrying out my every pleasureful command.

His skin at the end of my leather crop... *Oh, the moans I could get from him.* I noticed the way his eyes dilated as I moved in closer to him... so responsive to my presence.

I could make him come without even a touch.

Thrills of excitement shoot through me as I recall him in the locker room, butt-ass naked, water dripping off his freshly cleaned muscular form. Distracting, to say the least, and *entirely* impressive. With the equipment he plays with, I know I won't be disappointed.

The pressure between my legs builds as I turn the corner, gripping my steering wheel a little too tightly when the gravelly road creates friction between my skin and the tight jeans.

Knock it off, Sable. You don't have time to take care of those thoughts tonight.

Gabby, my best friend, hooked us up with a VIP table at one of the hottest nightclubs in Hollywood to celebrate my birthday. Daydreaming about Matt's pain tolerance and foreplay will have to wait.

Once I reach my condo, I run upstairs to change. A month ago, I had picked up this blood-red micro mini and have been dying to wear it. The top is a halter, which slips over my head and drapes seductively down, showing off my cleavage. A thin black belt accents my tiny waist. My black, four-inch Jimmy Choo heels add to my five-eleven height and accentuate my legs even more.

My phone buzzes, drawing my attention away from the mirror. I pick it up and see Gabby is out front in the sleek black town car she ordered for the night. Taking one last quick look, I pick up my bag and strut out the door.

As soon as the driver opens the back door, she yells, "Happy Birthday, Bitch!" As our tradition dictates, she hands me a banner to wear that reads "Birthday Bitch" across it, then we pop a bottle of champagne.

"Cheers, Bitch! Let's cut loose tonight and have some fucking fun!" I announce.

Gabby holds her glass up to make a toast. "Here's to getting you laid tonight."

"What the hell? I'm just fine in that area." My eyes meet Gabby's.

Despite knowing what I do for money while I chase my dream job, Gabby looks at me wide-eyed. "What? Battery-operated doesn't count. We are talking about a live cock. Girl, if you're getting laid and you aren't sharing the details, I will be pissed. The only stories I've heard lately are men that want to be spanked not fucked."

I laugh at her. "Worry about your own love life."

Thank goodness we pull up in front of the club and the driver opens the door to let us out. The entry line wraps around the corner, but Gabby has the hookup. We sashay right up to the bouncer. Gabby gives her name, the door is immediately opened, and we are escorted to our VIP table upstairs on the second story, right above the dance floor.

The music pounds as if keeping in beat with my heart. Colored lights bounce off the floor, accenting the elaborate styles of everyone on the dance floor. There is no pressure of everyday life. Tonight is all about celebrating, relaxing, and having fun.

"Gabby, I don't know how to thank you for all this. This location is amazing. We can see everyone." I lean over and hug her once we are seated. The upstairs is set up with round plush black couches and is in direct view of the main bar. I see the four bartenders expertly taking care of anyone that walks up as they flirt and move with the music. It's the perfect location because we can carry on conversations but still enjoy the music.

"You're welcome; it worked out perfectly for both of us. Dante Delucchi, the club owner, has been trying to get me to come and do a piece on his club since it opened." Gabby has a very successful online blog and podcast about the hippest places, which makes her popular among the rich and famous.

After a round of drinks, Gabby drags us onto the dance floor; DJ Mixmaster is spinning tonight. The music is thumping. The beat is driving everyone to their feet.

We are in the middle of our fifth straight song when DJ Mixmaster announces, "Ladies and Gentlemen, put your hands together for Matt Jones, our hometown hero and two-time MMA USA Heavyweight Champion."

The club goes wild, cheering for Matt as I watch him and his entourage, being led to the area next to ours. We lock eyes for an instant. Matt has forgotten the two women he had his arms around as he stands to watch Gabby and I dance. His eyes are glued to us, the two ladies are clearly not happy with the lack of attention, even if only for a moment. They tug Matt toward their waiting area.

Eddie follows Matt's eyes and spots me. I see him lean over to one of Matt's securities saying something to him as he points his finger toward me on the dance floor.

I can't help laughing that an MMA Champion needs security to protect him from me. *He's not going to ruin my fun;* I think to myself and continue to dance. After a few minutes, I need a drink and to give my feet a much-needed rest. I tap Gabby on the shoulder, indicating I'm going up to rest and get a drink.

Gabby and I worm our way through the crowd, passing Matt's table on the way. He's surrounded by females all willing to fulfill his *vivid imagination.*

He had balls, I'll give him that, but he thought he could intimidate me with his statement. Maybe at seventeen, when I was homeless and lost, he would have, but now, I'm far from the scared naïve girl I was when I first met Ms. Sally.

He has no idea how vivid my imagination can get when I want it to. I did my research on him, in and out of his persona. Rumors surround him, about his connection with BDSM and his dominate ways. I had my doubts, but they must be true given the position of the two women that walked in on his arm, or more specifically the way the practically kneeled at his side.

22

"Look how cute, Gabby... Twin bookends." I point to the two submissive women at Matt's feet while looking him in the eye. I walk past him, laughing.

Matt reaches out and grabs my arm.

Stopped dead in my tracks, with a firm hold from him and my quivering thighs, I cock my head to the side and lift my brows in question. Though, there's not a single doubt on his face—

He wants me.

The tension in his silent mouth says it loud and clear. But it's the slant of his eyes, the darkness in them, the way they barely blink in my presence that says it all. He'd throw me up against that wall and have his way with me, in front of all these people, if he could.

But he can't. Not yet. And that's what makes this fun. He doesn't know it yet, but I'm not a bookend, and I don't tend to give away samples of my services for free.

I smile as our eyes meet, and I guide them to his hold on my person. Neither had I given him permission to touch me, nor had I asked for it, yet I don't seem to mind the connection. The burning heat where his hand touches my skin, like an electric current directly to my core. I don't want the current to end.

His thumb gently caresses my skin. "You won't be laughing when I have you submitting to me. I'm going to enjoy punishing a brat like you."

"Me? Submitting? You better be sure you're Dom enough to attempt something like that with an experienced woman," I whisper in Matt's ear, allowing my lips to gently brush his earlobe. I inhale his scent before jerking my arm away from his grip.

Gabby waves at Eddie Langley and another man. *Shit, what the hell is she up to?* I think to myself as the two join us.

"Dante, this is my friend, Sable," Gabby introduces us. "It's her birthday; we are celebrating tonight."

Dante is a nice-looking man— totally the type of man Gabby would fall for. Stylishly dressed from head to toe. Loves the attention of the public and people fawning over him. His dark hair is perfectly styled, and he wears silk pants and a dark blue jacket with a white button-up shirt. As he stands next to Gabby, they look as if they belong on the cover of a GQ magazine.

"Very nice to meet you. Your club is killer. Thank you for hooking us up," I tell him.

"You ladies are on my permanent list. You're welcome anytime and will always have a table. I can't go wrong with two gorgeous women such as you two attending my place."

"That's very generous, Dante, thank you. Would you like to join us for a drink?" I ask him as I motion for him to have a seat.

"I'd be honored. I need to send one quick message." He pulls out his phone and types in something.

Instantly, the music volume turns down as DJ Mixmaster picks up the microphone. "I would like to have everyone's attention. Dante would like everyone to raise their glasses to toast a happy birthday to Sable Wagner."

A spotlight appears on me, and everyone in the club begins to cheer and clap. Four waitresses walk up, carrying a magnum of champagne, glasses, and a cake that took two people to bring. Everyone breaks into singing the happy birthday song to me.

I can't believe Gabby has done all this for me. She is more than my best friend; Gabby is family. I only have a couple of people in my life I'm close to and Gabby is definitely one of them.

I raise my glass and hold it out to everyone to toast them, then hug Gabby, and of course, Dante.

Then I hear, "Do I get a hug too?"

Goosebumps break out across my skin. I can't let him see what he does to me, so I slip back into reporter mode.

Matt wears the same clothes I watched him put on a few hours ago. I know damn well he is bare under those tight-fitting jeans. I fight the need to let my eyes slide down his body and respond, "Of course, you can if you would like one, Mr. Jones."

Gabby bumps my arm. "We don't have to be so formal tonight, Sable; none of us are working, are we, Matt? I'm Gabby, the best friend."

Matt reaches his hand out to Gabby. "Forgive me for crashing your celebration." His eyes scan the sash across my chest. "I just came over to say happy birthday." He takes Gabby's hand and kisses the knuckles, but never takes his eyes off me.

Dante comes to stand next to me. "Matt, this is Sable Wagner."

Matt takes my hand and does the same as he did to Gabby's. His eyes never leave mine. "I feel as if we have met before," he says with a smirk.

"Are you sure you can spare the time away from your night's entertainment?" I look at the next seating area to see the two women clearly pouting.

I lean into him and whisper, "Your bookends look lonely."

Gabby jumps in. "You two haven't met, but I think you should. Please join us." She points to the seat next to where I had been seated.

"What makes you think Sable and I should meet, Gabby?" Matt takes the drink offered to him, leans back, puts his arm on the cushion behind me, gives me a quick wink, and then looks at Gabby.

"Well, you're an amazing fighter, and Sable is an outstanding reporter. If you need another reason?"

Gabby raises her glass to the two of us. "You look hot sitting next to each other."

"I can't argue with her logic," I say with a giggle. Fuck being in reporter mode. I've had just enough to drink that I'm relaxed and having a good time. And the only thing I can focus on is the way I felt on the way home tonight. The way he made me feel. It had been a long time since I had been in the submissive role. And it was probably some of the greatest years of my life.

Matt slides closer to me, his muscular thigh covered in denim. The rough material rubs against my bare skin. His hand leaves the back of my seat to slowly draw small circles down my naked spine.

He does like touching me without permission. If there ever was a Dom to unlock my switch Matt would be the one.

"You know what it's going to take to get an interview with me, sweetheart. Whenever you're ready, have Dante give me a call." He leans in and gives me a quick kiss on the lips. "Happy Birthday, Princess."

"If that peck is supposed to turn me on, Matt, I have news for you: That's how a woman expects to be kissed by their grandfather. That's not a kiss to turn me on, or cause me to want to fuck you senseless."

"Are you ready to give me what I want, Princess?" He stands, grinning at me. "When you're ready to get on your knees, I'll show you what kind of man I am."

The nerve of that man. I squeeze my thighs together, trying to get some relief from the saturated material between my folds. I stand and call him to turn around, "Matt! I'm not a princess. I'm a fucking Queen. I don't get on my knees for no man. They bow for me."

My friend is at my side instantly. "You fucking tell him, Sable."

Gabby puts her arm around my shoulder. "Damn, you could have some fun with that one."

I laugh and nod my head in agreement. She has no idea the kind of fun I have been thinking of all evening since seeing him in a towel. I quickly take a drink to try to cool off.

It doesn't help.

Fuck, I need some relief, I think to myself. "Gabby let's go dance and see

what kind of mischief we can find ourselves in."

"Now you're talking girl." Gabby takes my hand as we prance out to the dance floor adding extra sway to our hips with each step.

I can feel his eyes on me as I grind against a willing participant on the dance floor. Lifting my hair off my neck as I turn to face my dance partner, I straddle his thigh and grind against his muscular body.

I risk a glance in Matt's direction. His eyes bore down on me. I'm dancing for him; never have I wanted a man to want me as much as I do Matt at this moment.

three

MATT

As I ADJUST MY COCK WITHOUT ANYONE SEEING, I GO BACK TO my table and sit down. A hard-on and tight jeans aren't a comfortable combination, but that seems to be the outcome of being in the same room as Sable.

I stand, watching the show Sable puts on while dancing. I know her performance is for me. I have never wanted to go grab a woman, throw her over my shoulder, and carry her out the door, straight to the first bed I can find.

Her sass, strength... Sable oozes sex appeal.

I order a shot of tequila, and before the waitress gets too far away, I stop her and tell her to bring the bottle and enough glasses for us all.

Eddie sits next to me. "What's wrong? You don't usually do shots."

"Nothing... Just feeling anxious. Get rid of the bookends. I don't want to mess with amateurs tonight," I tell him. "I don't feel like dealing with anyone."

"What do you need me to do?" Eddie puts his hand on my shoulder. "I can call the club and have them send other girls over to your house if that's what you want. I can tell them exactly what you need."

"Find out everything you can about Sable Wagner. I want to know it all."

Eddie looks out on the dance floor toward Sable and shakes his head. "You're not considering getting involved with the rookie reporter, are you?" Eddie asks. "The last time you did something like this it cost you a hundred grand do I need to remind you?"

"Let it go, you got paid for your work." By the look of his clothes and shoes, he gets paid very well for his work for me.

Eddie unbuttons his suit jacket to span his arms over the spine of the booth.

"It's not about the compensation, Matt. You know that."

I do. Eddie earns every percentage he gets from me.

"It's about women like that taking your head out of the game. There are big things in the works, things we have been working toward since we first started out." Eddie sits up and points toward Sable and Gabby. "They're pretty to look at but remember that story almost destroyed your career? How did it set back all the hard work you have done?"

I'm not in the mood to rehash the same old conversation again and I don't want to have it thrown up in my face. "Right. My hard work."

"What do you always say? *A good fuck isn't worth an entire career.*" He holds both hands up. "Your words, not mine man."

We both glance at the bookends.

"I promised you a steady supply, and I've always delivered. You promised me NDAs and focus." He flicks his wrist and the girls get up and leave. He then sends a message on his phone before saying, "So I just want to make sure you think-since thinking isn't really, you're thing."

"Fuck you..."

"You asked what I needed, just do what I tell you to do!" I snap at him, then instantly feel like shit for doing it. He always gets the brunt of my moods when I need to release some of my pent-up adrenaline after a fight. I'll apologize to him later.

Eddie gets up and walks off, taking the two bookends with him. A moment later, the two professional ladies from the limo join me. One on each of my sides, they are making it very clear I will be well taken care of as soon as I permit them to proceed. They have partied with me several times and are very familiar with my Dom style and my needs.

Sable is still on the dance floor with her friend Gabby. I can't take my eyes off her. She raises her long black hair off her back and neck to cool off, showing her bare spine and how low her dress dips down.

While Dante and another guy dance with Sable and Gabby, I lick my lips as I imagine running my hands over her body and wrapping her hair around my hand to control her as I bend her over.

Instead of me, the guy she dances with slides his hands down her sides, stopping as he reaches her hips. She turns her back to him, swinging her hips as she rubs against his crotch, teasing and coaxing the man as she leans back against his chest.

He leans down and says something in her ear, causing Sable to smile and close her eyes. She lets him lead the motion of their bodies together with the rhythm of the music.

I can't watch it anymore. Not when I'm not the one touching her.

I've never had such a reaction to a woman. Sable is definitely someone I will continue to get to know one way or another. I send Eddie a quick text apologizing for being a dick and telling him I'm taking the car but leaving my two playmates behind for the evening. I'm not in the right head space to play with anyone tonight.

I march off toward the door. My two-security details follow me out and ensure I make it to the car without any issues from the fans.

By the time I'm dropped off at home, I have calmed down and am glad I called it an early evening. I step into the house, not bothering to turn on any lights. I head upstairs to the bedroom. After stripping off my clothes, I flop on the bed to enjoy the coolness of the Egyptian sheets against my skin.

Sending those two women home hasn't solved the problem of my hard-on. Just the thought of Sable on the dance floor, raising the hair off her back causes me to go rock hard.

My phone dings with a text from Eddie—a report about Sable.

Shit. It only says the name and address, all the basics. The only job it lists is a freelance sports reporter.

She wants to use me to make a name for herself. Eddie is right, the last thing I need to do is get mixed up with her. I toss my phone on the bed next to me.

Damn, that information doesn't even mention family or anything.

I can't fault Eddie though, especially since I had never asked him to dig up information on a non-fighter before. It's easy to learn someone in the ring, study their moves, predict them, and adapt to them.

Now I'm inquisitive. It's as if Sable Wagner didn't

exist until five years ago. I find one piece of information very handy and that's her address.

I turn on my back and wait for sleep to come, but instead, my mind drums up a reason to stay awake.

A daydream featuring Sable.

A porn mind scene.

She stands in front of me, desire filling her dark eyes as her tongue slides across her bottom lip. The same one she bites, causing my cock to grow hard.

"On your knees, Sable!" I command the figment of her, but she doesn't do as I say.

Instead, her lips part slightly, then she smirks. "You better learn how to be a Dom before you try that with an experienced woman."

I quickly grab her by the back of the neck, fisting my hand in her hair. My mouth assaults hers. Our tongues duel. A moan escapes from her as my hand slides between her legs, forcing her thighs apart. Sliding my fingers inside her panties I can feel the moistness and heat emitting from her core.

I snap out of it with a raging hard-on and sweating as if I had just finished a workout. A single thought surfaces, *Could Sable be the experienced woman I have been craving?*

I need to learn more about Sable, I decide. She wants an interview. Maybe I should see just how badly she wants one.

My phone rings. I grab it from the nightstand beside the bed. I see it's Eddie.

"You're calling early," I tell him, even though it's after ten a.m. At some point, my daydream had turned into sleeping.

"This call couldn't wait. I received a call from Oratorio Salvador's manager."

I sit up on the edge of my bed. Eddie now has my attention. Oratorio is the World Heavyweight Champion. "What did he want?"

"They want a title fight between you and Oratorio? In eight months, in LA."

"What did you tell him?" I try to remain calm. This would be the fight of my dream, World Champion.

"I had to see what your schedule looked like, and we would discuss it and get back to them in the next few days." Eddie sounds quite pleased with his response.

"Call them back and tell them to email all the information they have and any questions to us, and we will get back to them in forty-eight hours!" I bark at him.

"Matt, let me do my job. You don't want to sound too eager." Eddie is getting defensive with me.

"I want to see the information today!" I yell into the phone and hang up. Seriously, he is going to jack around, and they will withdraw the offer for the match.

"Matt..." Eddie walks into my home office a few minutes later.

"Do. It Now!"

"All right, all right, calm down." He shuts the door, and I hear him on the phone. A few minutes later, he walks back in, handing me some paperwork.

"You should have let me hold out for a bigger payout," he says. "Since when do you question the way, I do my job?"

I glance threw the papers and see that the fight is Labor Day in LA. The payout for losers will be two point five million. The winner is paid ten million. "There isn't a damn thing wrong with this payout. This is the fight I have always wanted, and you're trying to fuck it up by being greedy?" I walk over to the counter, grab a pen, and sign it. "Send it back to them." I push the papers toward Eddie. "I'm not questioning you doing your job, you know how long I have worked toward this fight. I can't risk anything or anyone fucking it up, even you."

"Man, you need to get laid," he states, picking up the papers. "You just won a major fight and are usually in a great mood. What the fuck is wrong with you?"

"I don't know," I confess I'm being a dick and not sure why. "I'm going down to the gym. Leave me alone for a while, let me work out this shitty mood. I'll talk to you next week."

"All right, man, let me know if you need anything." I hear the door close after he walks out.

I turn toward the bedroom to change for the gym when I see a business card lying on my counter. Picking it up, I read:

Club E...

Where fantasies come true, and you can experience what you didn't know you needed.

Flipping the card over, I see an address and nothing more.

four

SABLE

Deviating from my morning ritual throws my entire day off. Coffee and yoga are needed every morning to get myself mentally and physically prepared for my day.

Today, however, I couldn't reach my Zen during yoga. My mind kept going back to Matt. I replayed our interactions over and over in my mind.

After an hour, I give up and search for more coffee. Starting on my second cup of the day, I sit down at my laptop to write my article about Matt's fight, where he successfully defended his championship.

I know my editor is going to point out the fact I don't have a direct quote from Matt.

Leaning back in my desk chair, I reflect on my conversations with Matt to see if there is anything I can ethically use. Nothing comes to mind. I don't think my editor would appreciate the quote about his sexual appetite or how I could earn the interview. Honestly, he would probably wonder why I didn't just do it to get the interview.

I, on the other hand, can't quit thinking about Matt's offer or about what type of a Dom a man like Matt is. He clearly knows what he wants, but I wonder what he would do with another dominate? Like me.

The thought of dominating Matt causes my nipples to go hard.

My phone dings, letting me know I have a text message.

GABBY:

You need to call me now!

I quickly dial her. "What's up?"

"Have you turned your story in yet?" she asks.

"No."

"Eddie just told me Matt signed a contract with Oratorio Salvador for a title fight over Labor Day here in LA."

"No shit! I have to go, Gabby. I love you." I quickly hang up my phone and promptly type the information Gabby had just given me. I change the title of my article to '**Matt Jacob Goes for World Title.**'

After hitting send, I call my editor.

"Read it now," I say the second he picks up.

"Sable, are you positive about this?" my editor asks.

"His manager just told Gabby so she would spread it across the internet. She gave me the tip first."

"Great job." We are going to run this on the first page. "Follow up with both fighters and get interviews." He quickly hangs up without saying anything else.

I shoot Gabby a text.

ME:

The article's running. Have to interview both fighters. I'll figure that out later… I'm due at Club E in a couple of hours.

I walk to the bathroom, turn on the water, and fill my soaking tub. After pouring in some of my favorite orange blossom bubble bath, I step in front of my mirror and twist my hair into a bun on top of my head.

Returning to my tub, I strip, tossing my clothes in the corner hamper. I sit on the tub's edge, slowly dipping my toes into the hot water. I can't help but moan as I gently slide my body down. Taking a deep intake of air, I relish the way the water heats the soft, tender skin between my legs. My thighs squeeze tighter to protect the sensitive skin from the warmth.

After a moment of being submerged, I slowly open my legs wide, letting the comfort caress my sensitive skin, then gently swish my legs open and closed, teasing myself with the gentle waves. The water laps against my taut nub, which desperately needs some attention this evening.

I reach into the small table next to my tub, my fingers searching until I touch the latex object I have been looking for. I prop my left leg up on the side of the tub, pushing the button on the end of my pleasure machine. At pressing the button one more time, the head of the nine-inch massager, which I had nick-named Marcus, slowly twists in a slow circle while the length pulses in and out. Today *Marcus* isn't the right name for my massager, not when *Matt* fills my mind... So, I rename it.

I push the device inside, moaning as *Matt* sinks deeper, twisting and pumping as it slides further into my core. My release builds. Touching the button one more time, setting the speed on overdrive— *Matt* pounds in and out.

My release hits me quick and hard, causing my leg to loudly splash down into the water. Water sloshes over the edge of the tub and onto the floor.

"Damn," I roar to no one, then laugh at myself as I clean off *Matt*.

Once I finish bathing, I quickly put on shorts and a T-shirt. Club E requires a different attire, one I'll change into once I get there. This way I don't have to worry about running into someone I know while in my costume.

I'm not ashamed of being a Dominatrix. I love it, actually. If not for the fact that I will eventually become too old to be desirable in the sex industry, I wouldn't worry about another career, but sports reporter is my passion project ever since I got a taste for it in high school.

My high school principal, one of the people who inspired my sports reporter dream, had approached me about being on the school paper and covering the sports section. I didn't know anything about sports but having someone interested in what I had to say was uplifting. Knowing there was a man out there that believed I could truly be something other than a slut, like my mother, meant even more. He took the time to explain the game and rules of every sport to me. My research sparked a passion in me that I had never had before. People wanted to know what I had to say and I got to do something I loved. My principal and Ms. Sally made sure I graduated high school. Ms. Sally and some of the girls were there cheering me on as my family.

Realistically speaking, there would be no chance of me being a Sports reporter if my occupation got out.

In my dressing room, I slither into my thigh-high nylons, a garter, and a black leather lace-up body suit.

Over it, I slip on a long black leather skirt, which is split up on both sides, and top it off with five-inch, knee-high stiletto boots. I wear my hair braided and in a bun on top of my head and opt for bright red lipstick and a mask to hide my identity.

As soon as the mask slides into place, Sable no longer exists. I become Madame E.

I sit at my make-up table when the phone rings. No need to answer it, it's just an alarm, advising me that my client had arrived. From the two-way mirror directly in front of me, I watch him play with his glasses, rather impatiently.

I can't get a clear visual of his face because he's looking away. The longer he waits for me, the angrier he grows. Every second that ticks by adds to his nervousness.

Good.

Standing, I reach for the doorknob. Just as I open the door, the outer room door slams shut. Clearly, he had not been patient enough to wait.

No way was he ready to submit, I think to myself.

At least I won't have to deal with someone who thinks they know everything when really, they don't know shit. A walk-in, looking to learn, is more accessible to teach than trying to break the bad habits of someone who thinks they have everything under control.

With some time to spare, I tour the club to check on the other girls. I have been here longer than all of them, except for Ms. Sally, who owns the club. I peek into each studio, careful not to disturb the scene going on inside.

The girls tend to look up and smile if everything is fine. Otherwise, they will ask me to join them if they are having any issues with their guest.

In this building, I have learned a lot about human nature, emotions, and allowing oneself the ability to express their desires. I learned early on that there are dominates and submissive. I was even more surprised to learn about switches. I found quickly that with the right dominate, I'm quite at ease being a submissive. Given my past, I was taken back by this knowledge.

I turn to head back to my room when the front door opens. Perhaps my appointment had second thoughts and has decided to return, but the man looks up at the camera.

My breath catches. *Matt.*

Shit. I hide behind my door as if he can see me. It's ridiculous, but suddenly this leather has gotten tighter. I sneak a peek out of the room and immediately retreat.

Nope. Not my heart playing tricks on me. Matt is actually here. *I can hear my heartbeat in my ears. How in the world did he find me here?*

"Stop it, Sable," I say to myself

I rest my head against the door and shut my eyes—squeeze them so hard... as if they could expel the image of him...in my space... from my sight.

Does he know about me? My thoughts take off, trying to rationalize his presence.

I have never seen him here before. This probably means this is his first time and it can't be a coincidence.

How did he find out? Even if he did a background check on me, he wouldn't discovery anything. I hadn't used social media the entire time I was growing up, especially when I was staying with Ms. Sally. I didn't want my mother to track me, not that she ever decided to look for me.

As my dream career flashes before my eyes to the tune of my rapidly beating heart, I open my eyes and swear into the air.

Is the universe playing with me by sending him here? It's not like we are the only sex club in LA.

While our hostess talks to him, I buzz the front desk quickly. "Put the new guest in my studio," I tell her and hang up.

I watch as she has him sign all the confidentiality paperwork. I take a few deep breaths to gain control of my breathing before entering my studio. I've never had a fantasy about a man, then have him show up in my studio. I walk in ignoring the fact that I know who he is.

I have everything to lose if Club E is exposed as where I work.

"Good evening, what brings you to Club E tonight?" As soon as I speak, he turns to face me.

My voice. Crap.

A look of recognition crosses his features for a brief moment, then vanishes as his eyes trail the contours of my outfit.

Crisis averted.

I slowly walk past him, dragging my hand along his broad muscular shoulder. He tenses at my touch.

"I'm not quite sure. A friend gave me the card and I thought I would come and check it out."

"I see. Just so there is no misunderstanding, we are a sex club. We allow a person to experience their fantasy or curiosities without judgment."

"I gathered that much."

"Why do you think your friend sent you here?"

"I've been a dick to him lately, and he told me I needed to get laid."

I almost break character and laugh in agreement with the honesty of his statement. "Maybe you should apologize to him and anyone else you have been curt with."

Matt shrugs his shoulders. "Six to eight weeks of hard work outs and no sex gets frustrating. And I'm about to start the process again for my next fight, so here I am."

"That has to be very frustrating for you." I slink over and sit down on the end of the bed and look at him. I watch as he comes to sit next to me.

"May I?" he asks before sitting.

"Of course."

Matt sits so close to me, our thighs touching, but not his hands this time. Not even his eyes connect with mine. Seeing this side of Matt is endearing. He's not pushing to prove he's the best. It's as if he is at peace in his own skin and with the person he is.

"I have a few more questions if you don't mind. They allow me to get to know you and see if I'm the best person for you."

"You are," he responds right away.

"We might have someone else that is more suited to your tastes or your needs."

"How do you know my tastes?" he asks, shooting me a cocky smirk. "I have an interesting palette."

That's a bit more like the guy from my birthday. "Then you have come to the right place. We specialize in interesting palettes."

"That's for me to decide," I put him in his place. This is my room, my playground. "Let's start with something easy."

Matt bobs his head for me to continue.

"Do you think you are dominating, or are you submissive?" I ask him.

"I'm a Dom."

"Have you ever submitted?" I walk over to my toy chest and pick up a riding crop.

"No." Matt scans my body, his tone a bit more inviting than in our previous conversations.

"That's a shame," I whisper, just loud enough for him to hear despite the couple of feet between us.

His brows furrow at my comment, but his tongue doesn't move. Only his eyes. They fixate on the swishing of my thighs as I add more distance between us. I make my way toward the toy chest, near the dressing room.

"Wait," he asks. "Why is it a shame?" He stands striding toward me.

With my back to him, he doesn't see the smirk that crosses my lips, so I turn around and slide my fingers over the glazed wooden chest. "Well, you can't truly understand how to dominate until you have learned how to submit."

His head cocks to the side as he steps closer to me. "Says who?"

"Says someone with way more *experience* than you."

With his eyes fixated on my long legs, Matt takes a seat on the bench, spreading out his body to occupy most of it. "That's the second time someone has said something like that to me in twenty-four hours."

Crap. I busy my fingers by plucking the toy out of my box.

His shoulders are pulled back so tight, a single brush of my riding crop could make his posture snap.

But that would be too easy, so I move toward him and circle him. Reversing our earlier encounter, I position myself between his inner thighs. I reach out and stroke the side of his face with the riding crop. "If your submissive doesn't completely trust you and know that no matter what, they are safe with you, the relationship will never work for either participant."

"Trust," he echoes back. "I just got here and I don't even know you."

Maybe he doesn't know it's me. My heart muscles ease up a bit.

"This is a safe place. I'm here for you and with you... What do you need to trust me?"

"You." His eyes never leave mine. The tip of his tongue quickly slides across his bottom lip. "I want you to be my person here."

"That's not exactly how it works. You will be rewarded with your submission. The rewards are of my choosing. Having me doesn't mean you are going to have intercourse with me every time you come to the club."

"Can I pay extra to have you submit to me?" Matt asks, never taking his eyes off me.

"I am a switch, but I only submit to Doms I know are properly trained and that I feel comfortable with. I can tell you I will not be submitting to any Dom, even one as sexy as you, that doesn't know how to treat me the way I desire and deserve to be treated."

"So, you think I'm sexy?" Matt asks with a grin.

"You know very well that you are, which makes you an even more dangerous man."

He starts to stand. I touch his shoulder with the crop. "I didn't request that you stand."

"And I didn't agree to submit."

"You are correct." I saunter over and open the door to the studio. "If you follow me, I will show you out of the club." I wait for him to stand and walk out the door. "Well?"

"You didn't tell me to stand and leave the room," he says cockily.

"You may stand and leave." I amble over and whisper in his ear.

"When I come back, how do I ensure I'll get to see you?"

"You can call ahead and schedule a scene with Madame E, and they will let you know if I'm available. What name will you be using so I know who you are?"

"Matt Jacobs"

"Is that your real name?"

"Yes."

"Most men that come here use an alias."

"I'm not like most men. Besides, you all had me sign enough confidentiality papers when I came in the door to know my real name. I figure I'm safe." He stands and walks toward the door. I follow him.

He leans in, takes my hair in his hand, and holds it to his nose. After a quick sniff, he kisses me on the lips. "I'll see you again soon, Madame E. I can't wait to earn my rewards from you. Orange blossom is my favorite scent." He grins and strolls down the hall toward the reception area.

I stand outside the closed door for a moment, trying to get my breathing under control.

Maybe he did recognize me? *My voice. My shampoo.*

No. I'm just being paranoid. *Right?*

My head fills with all these questions, including how sexy it will be to see a man like Matt Jones on his knees in front of me.

I can't believe how turned on I am just from our conversation and all the thoughts of the scenes we have in our future.

Ms. Sally saunters down the hall. "You okay, sweetheart?" She is dressed in a long navy-blue negligee with a matching robe and heels. Her long blonde hair hangs loosely around her shoulders.

Though Ms. Sally is in her late sixties, she looks like she's in her forties. She is five foot ten inches, slender built.

"I'm not sure," I confess to her.

"Walk with me." We turn and head back toward her office, where I proceed to tell her all about my interactions with Matt outside Club E and end with our little run-in a few moments ago.

"That's some story. Are you sure Gabby didn't send him here?" she asks.

I quickly grab her desk phone and dial Gabby to ask.

Gabby answers, "No way, girl, I wouldn't do that to you. Whip his ass and make him give you that interview," she says before I hang up.

Ms. Sally laughs at hearing Gabby's suggestion. "I've always liked that girl."

Ms. Sally sits at her computer, typing away, then stops. "Matt Jones called in earlier today and booked the appointment himself. He put Eddie Langley down as his reference."

"That's his manager."

"Eddie has been a client here for over a year. He's a regular of a couple of the other girls."

"That solves the mystery; it's a coincidence." I walk over to the bar and pour each of us a glass of wine. "Do you think I need to hand Matt over to someone else?"

"Someone else?" Ms. Sally leans back on her chair

and grips the arm rests as she angles toward me. "I've never seen you react to a man the way you are this one."

"He's ..." I trail off because I don't even know how to explain it. Ms. Sally is the one person who I should be able to be honest with. She has taught me to trust people and my instincts, my sexuality. Most importantly, she's taught me self-worth.

Ms. Sally taught me how to be a submissive allowing me to watch and learn as she trained and worked with her clients. She then taught me how to be a dominatrix. Years of watching her play and then graduating to take on my own clients I realized I enjoyed being a switch.

As Ms. Sally trained me, she also took on a motherly role toward me. We never had a sexual relationship. I could talk to her about anything as I could with any of the other girls.

Ms. Sally always pushed me to go after my dream of being a sports caster. She made sure I finished school and attended college. All the things a real mother would have done.

The most important lesson Ms. Sally taught me was: In a dominate, submissive relationship the submissive has all the power. The submissive controls, how intense the scene gets, what the hard limits are, and if the scene needs to stop.

As Ms. Sally's submissive, we never had a sexual

relationship. Not every submissive relationship is sexual, some are based on love and mental health. Some are not about sexual attraction or defining preference, at least not at Club E. Club E offers something unique. It goes beyond sexual preference, beyond attraction, if it needs to.

What Ms. Sally and I had was complicated and yet exactly what I needed at the time. Beyond what she did for me and showing up for me, she introduced me to a secure space. Instilled a sense of peace in me just by taking control.

During a scene, I could relinquish all control to Ms. Sally— in her hands, I was worry-free. I wasn't just a homeless girl with mommy issues, I was worthy. I was fierce and powerful, and unafraid. And outside of a scene, when the panic would set in and the feelings took over, she used her Dom role to keep me from losing myself.

Were Ms. Sally and I romantically involved? No, but I love her. I appreciate her, and I look up to her. I did then, and I still do. I'm honored to have been her submissive.

I learned to watch people to ensure that they were telling me the truth that they have reached their limits and to know when it was just nerves feeding their fear.

"I would see where it goes. If he gets too close to figuring out who you are or you don't think you can handle him, just let me know and I'll make sure you don't have to deal with him anymore." She squeezes my hand. "Your next appointment has just been canceled. It looks like you have the night off."

"I'm going to change and work on getting some interviews set up." I give Ms. Sally a hug and a quick kiss on the cheek. "Thanks for always being here."

"Always, sweetie. Goodnight."

I go back to my dressing room and change into my street clothes. I call Gabby again. "I'm headed to your house, should be there in twenty minutes. I need to find a way to get these interviews. Do you know anyone on the Oratorio Salvador's team?"

"Let's see what I can find out." I hear Gabby typing feverishly on her keyboard. She relays information back to me as she uses her computer skills to dig up some information. Eventually, I hang up. Not really sure if she realizes it or not, but when I arrive at her house, Gabby meets me at the door and drags me to her laptop to show me her post.

I read it aloud, "Looking to speak to anyone that can help my girl Sable get in touch with Oratorio Salvador. If he wants to have his side heard, first reach out on any upcoming events he has going on."

Within ten minutes, Gabby has a message from Oratorio's publicist, wanting my contact information. The excitement takes over, and I jump up and down and yell in Gabby's living room. I can't believe everything I have worked so hard for is coming true.

Oratorio's publicist sends me a text telling me Oratorio would love to do an interview.

I quickly respond that I will be in touch with her to get it set up.

Gabby sends my information, and we both wait for my phone to ding. After an hour, our excitement deflates as we sit on the couch, not saying a word to each other.

I gather my things, ready to call it a night when my phone goes off. I look at the screen and sit back on the couch, not saying anything. Gabby keeps asking me what it says, as I carry out the conversation with Matt, who for some reason thinks he can dictate who I speak to.

"What is it?" Gabby asks at my pout. I don't answer, just hand the phone to her while I review what I had written over her shoulder. "Are you sure he didn't know it was you at Club E?"

MATT:

> You're seriously going to interview Oratorio before me?

ME:

> Unlike you, I'm sure he will respect me and my job. Not expect anything from me but to be treated fairly and to be heard.

A minute later, I get a response.

MATT:

> I behaved like an ass and would like to apologize. Can we have dinner while you and I talk?

ME:

> Rondo's, on the pier at eight p.m. tomorrow night? I'll make the reservation in my name.

MATT:

> I'll be there.

ME:

> Wait, one more thing… how did you get my number?

MATT:

> I have good friends too.

How had he gotten my number? I slowly raise my head from staring at my phone to my best friend, "Gabby, what did you do?"

"I… Okay, fine… I went out with Dante the other night, and we talked about how perfect you and Matt would be for each other. So, I gave him your number."

"Did you tell him about Club E?"

"Gawd, no! I wouldn't do that to you," she replies, shaking her head. "What did the text messages say?"

"He wants to have dinner, so I can interview him

before I speak to Oratorio." I start to gather my things to leave.

"Where are you going?"

"I have to research and have my questions down before tomorrow night." I give Gabby a quick hug. "Thank you for always having my back."

"Always... talk to you tomorrow."

I leave Gabby's and stop to pick up my favorite Chinese before driving the few blocks home. I unlock the door to my place, and Moose meets me, meowing loudly. I empty my arms of all the items I had been carrying and pick up my favorite creature on earth: Moose, my Chartreux cat. He has sky-blue eyes with gray-tipped ears. The rest of his fur is white, except for the gray on the muzzle of his face.

I found him when he was only a few weeks old out front of my house in the rain. I brought him in and took care of him. Since then, we became inseparable. I tell Moose my deepest secrets and never have to worry about him telling anyone.

While waiting for my computer to boot up, I pour myself a glass of wine and take a seat on the couch. I pull my legs up under me while taking a bite of my barely warm lo mein noodles.

I research the stats of both fighters and am surprised to see they are evenly matched, except for the two fights that have gotten Oratorio to be the World Champion.

Less than five pounds separate the two men. Oratorio has a two-inch shorter arm reach than Matt.

I look at the two men's photos and both are attractive. I'm instantly drawn to Matt's photo, though. His dark eyes are full of mystery needing to be unlocked. The thought of his beard against my inner thighs causes me to clench my legs together to ease the tension I instantly feel. His chiseled jaw gives him a hardened look, but I have seen firsthand, that when he is joking around a small dimple appears on his right cheek when he is laughing and completely relaxed.

five

MATT

Those eyes. That body. That voice. Madame E or Sable?

I can't get over the idea that one woman reminded me of the other.

My imagination is going into overdrive thinking the two women are the same person. Her scent of orange blossom is my favorite. I wonder if that is on the internet somewhere.

I grab my laptop and begin to google myself and read all the stories about me. I have gone down a rabbit hole of information looking for some hint that she used that scent to get to me.

There is nothing. I have never mentioned how I have come to love that smell to anyone.

I have to know if it's her, yet everything about Sable warns me to stay away. She's a reporter, gorgeous, sexy, intelligent, confident, and the type of woman to make a man go against every rule he has ever set for himself.

Kicking back, I relax on my couch and listen to jazz music playing in the background. Someone knocks at the door; I get up to answer it and find Eddie and Dante.

"What the fuck are you doing, going to dinner and interviewing with Sable?" Eddie yells at me as they enter the house

"I know what I'm doing, Eddie." I'm not sure if I'm trying to convince Eddie or myself of this.

"Do you guys want a beer?" I ask, walking into the kitchen.

"Sure," they say in unison.

"What are you two doing today, besides busting my chops?"

"We... well, I wanted to know if you went to Club E?" Eddie asks. "I was telling Dante about it and thought you might enlighten him on your visit."

"I just don't know if I'm ready to pay someone for sex," Dante admits.

"If you're going to a place like Club E, they take precautions to make sure everything is confidential. You have to sign a Non-Disclosure before you even see someone. You don't have to worry about anything getting on the internet." Eddie assures him.

Dante nods his head in agreement. "That's a plus."

"So how many times have you been there, Eddie?" I ask him. The thought of my best friend having sex with Madame E causes my anger to grow. The thought of any man paying to have sex with Sable, if she is Madame E, is more than I can stand to think of.

"Well, did you go?" Eddie pushes.

"No, I haven't been there." I lie, not wanting this conversation to continue any further. "Hey, I don't want to rush you out of here, but I was about to go into the gym and train when you arrived."

"Hey, no problem." Dante shakes my hand, standing to leave.

Eddie puts his hand on my shoulder. "Matt rethink doing this interview with Sable."

"The last time you took a reporter out to dinner, you ended up having a sexual relationship with her," Dante reminds me as he grabs his jacket.

Eddie points to Dante as a way of telling me to pay attention. I don't particularly like my past mistakes being thrown in my face. I glare at both of them, hoping they catch on that they are pushing it.

Dante continues despite Eddie's weird movements. "I'm not sure what he's doing, but I'm just trying to help you out. You let her in and she invaded your privacy—"

"Blasted it all over social media!" Eddie interjects as

he comes closer toward Dante. "Cost you a bunch of money and a payout to get her to retract the story."

"She didn't get me," I mumble. I just want these two assholes out of my house.

"She was about to get you in a lot of trouble," Dante warns. "She had a three-part story and she was going to go on some talk show to expose you."

I glare at Dante. I'm well aware the last reporter had plans of charging me for aggression. She was drunk and I was stupid. I let her in to my bedroom and tied her up, with her permission. She struggled.

"She took pictures," Eddie intervened again, pointing to his wrists.

"Sable won't do that. I'm not stupid enough to end up doing the same thing twice."

"I know what I'm doing."

"No, you don't."

"You're right, I don't, but she is interviewing Oratorio, so I should be interviewed."

Eddie begins to laugh. "Shut the fuck up."

"I'll talk to you later." I push him toward the door. *I love that guy. He always has my back and calls me out on my shit.*

Realizing I'm going to have to do something else to relax, I head into my home gym. After my first big win, I bought my house and furnished my personal gym with state-of-the-art equipment. Sometimes I just need to work out my thoughts without dealing with the public at a regular gym.

The endorphins from my workout are like a drug. My mood lightens, and when I stop for air, it's been two hours.

I jump in the shower, thinking about how to keep myself guarded tonight against the questions Sable will ask me. I know I will have to give her some information, but do I let her in completely?

No. She hides things too. Like working at a sex club. *Maybe.*

I look at the clock, realizing I have wasted most of the afternoon doing nothing. I go into the bathroom and pick up my laundry hamper to start a load of clothes. I grab the laundry soap and smell it. *Orange Blossoms.* The smell takes me back to my childhood, a special time in my life.

The same smell Madame E had.

I need to get ready to meet Sable at the restaurant. She wouldn't let me pick her up— maybe to make it clear that this, to her, is not a date.

Strictly professional, I think to myself.

At a restaurant, I doubt my initial thought. *Just the two of us and a recorder.*

Trying to keep it on her terms and the ball in her court will test my patience, but if Madame E is Sable,

I'll need to let her lead. She needs to trust me to respect her wishes.

Sable sits at the bar, looking gorgeous in her jeans and T-shirt with a photo of Pink on it. Her hair is in loose ringlets down her back.

Before I can make my approach, a guy takes the bar stool next to her, trying to initiate conversation.

She shakes her head, and just like that, the guy gets up and walks off. I can't help but chuckle to myself. She has a way of drawing men to her without even trying. Madame E may know how sexy she is, and know how to wield that into power, but the real Sable doesn't know how gorgeous she is.

I walk up to her, and without saying anything, take the seat beside her. I'm disappointed when I smell vanilla and not the same citrus smell of Madame E.

She doesn't even look at me. "That seat is taken."

"I hope it's for me," I answer.

She turns and smiles. "Right on time. I'm impressed." She picks up her purse from the bar and stands.

The hostess arrives. "Your table is ready, Mr. Jones."

"Thank you." I step aside and let Sable go first. We

order a glass of wine and take the menus from the waitress.

"Thank you for allowing me to interview you," Sable says, looking over the top of her menu with those beautiful eyes.

"You have some very influential friends to find out about the fight before the ink on the contract is even dry," I reply.

"I told you, I'm serious about being a Sports reporter," she says without looking at me. "Maybe you have someone in your corner that wants to make sure you get the publicity this fight deserves."

"Eddie." I can't help grinning at the thought. He's giving me hell for this interview and he's the reason for it.

Her not apologizing for going after her dream is a significant turn-on for me. When the waitress returns to take our orders, I am pleasantly surprised; I'm used to women ordering half-salads, dressing on the side, and barely picking at it, but not Sable. She orders the surf and turf, medium rare, with a loaded baked potato.

Everything I had planned on not telling Sable, I tell her. I told her about growing up with a father who was nothing— a man who couldn't hold a job or care for his family. It's not really that he couldn't. It's he wouldn't. He didn't care. I even tell her about a six-year-old me, on the day my mother left and didn't bother to take me with her.

Sable's eyes round at the thought of me abandoned by both parents.

"What was your family like?" I ask Sable.

She dodges my question. "The interview is about you, not me."

"Sucks..." I sum it up for her and take a sip of my wine. "I can afford it all now." I look around at the restaurant I had chosen for our non-date. "But as a kid, I had to steal to get even a small amount of food to eat." I slide the stem of the wine glass between my fingers as I watch the liquid swish back and forth. "Have you ever stolen?" The question comes out without me even thinking, but before I can excuse her from answering, she holds up a finger.

"Once, when I was starving. After my mom kicked me out of her house." She softly fists her hand and rests it on the table. "So... I get not wanting to repeat your childhood as an adult."

I nod but only because the palpitations in my chest keep me from speaking. After a few swallows and a good look at Sable, at a different side of her, I add, "You do whatever you can to break the cycle." She smirks softly, and I take a sip of my wine and clear my throat. "At least, that's what people say, right?"

She grabs the glass of her wine with her free hand. "You were saying about stealing?"

"Right... I was pretty scrawny. Insufficient nourishment and neglect have a way of making a kid feel out of place."

Her eyes soften, and for the first time tonight, puts down her pen. "You learned to take care of yourself at an early age?" Sable reaches over, placing her hand on my arm.

I nod and swallow the ball of emotion lodged in my throat. "My clothes were always dirty. I would do my best to wash them in the kitchen sink without any soap, but it never quite got out the stains." I glance at her again, she's looking at me the same way the person who changed my life had. Not with pity but understanding. With dignity.

"And how did you get out of that situation? Or did you stay?" Some people would probably be offended by the question, but from the way her shoulders had slumped, I think it was genuine curiosity.

"After a couple of years, I had a second-grade teacher who saw me—*really saw me*. She called social services, and they came to the house a few days later. Dad hadn't been home for a week or so. The social worker and police looked through the house while I sat on the couch with the nice lady who smelled clean..." I cut myself off before I let her in on that little piece of information.

I'll never forget the scent of cleanliness—of peace. I remember asking her what that smell was, and she told me it was just her shampoo and laundry detergent. I had her write down what she used to ensure I always had that smell with me.

"Did they put you into the system after that?"

"Yeah... That same day, I was placed into foster care that day. I was one of the lucky kids."

To take the focus off of me for a moment and to try and understand Eddie's report on why Sable seemed to have come out of nowhere five years ago, I ask, "What about you? What were you like as a kid?"

She bites on her bottom lip and then forces a smile. "I wasn't scrawny," she says with a coy smile. "I matured early, but my mom was more into herself and whatever man she met, than me. I left home for my safety and lived on the streets until someone found me, gave me a safe place to stay, and a job."

"Our childhoods aren't so different." Maybe the circumstances that brought us to where we are now are, but our traumas are similar.

"We both became cynical smartasses as a way to protect ourselves from the shit going on in our real lives is what I have concluded," Sable says, then begins to laugh.

I hold up my glass. "To being cynical smartasses."

We clink our glasses together. We laugh so much the table next to us calls the restaurant manager over to complain.

We laugh louder when he says he's sorry patrons enjoying their evening are disruptive to them. He then walks over with a bottle of wine and tops our glasses again personally.

We thank him and his staff for their excellent service and for allowing us to stay until closing. I leave a very generous tip with instructions that it is to be divided among all the staff.

Tonight, Sable brought out the best in me. I haven't seen this side of myself in years. It's nice not to be Matt Jones, MMA Champion. Instead, I was Matt Jones, a regular guy out for dinner with a friend, and I happened to be an MMA fighter as my job.

The town car is outside waiting for us as we exit the restaurant. "Can I give you a ride home?" I ask her, not wanting the evening to end.

"My car is right there across the street." She raises her arm, pointing toward a little red convertible.

"Nice car."

"Thank you; It was the first car I bought myself when I turned twenty-one," Sable responds, smiling proudly.

"You can tell you take good care of her."

Sable puts her hand on her hip, cocking it out to the side. "Why do all men assume that cars are women?"

"Honestly, I don't know." I shrug my shoulders and laugh. "Maybe the sexy lines of the car remind us of the curves of a woman's body?"

Her body.

"Damn, Matt, I like that." She places her hand on my forearm. A warmth fills my chest at her touch. "Did you just make that up?" She smiles at me.

"Hey, I haven't been hit in the head that often; I can still think independently."

Sable breaks out into a full belly laugh. I take her hand and start to walk her across the street.

When we reach the car, I release her hand and brush her hair back out of her face. "Are you going to make it home, all right?"

"Yes, thank you for a fun evening?"

"Would you have dinner with me again, not as a work dinner but as a date?"

"I think I would like that." She leans in and kisses me softly on my cheek. "Good night, Matt."

"Good night, Sable." I stand there, watching her drive away. I'm instantly lonely since she pulled away.

six

SABLE

I LIE AWAKE, REPLAYING MY EVENING WITH MATT IN MY MIND and hoping he had been honest with me tonight. I have no reason to doubt him, though. He showed me a different side at dinner, one I kind of understand. Matt plays a character on stage, much like me with Madame E, except I don't know where his persona ends and the real him starts.

When we first met, he was an arrogant, egotistical, selfish man who wanted all women to drop to their knees in his presence, but tonight... Tonight he was kind, confident, honest, and so sexy.

Matt oozes sexual energy. When he took my hand as he walked me across the street, I was instantly taken back to Club E. Seeing the lust in his eyes with the way he looked at me. Just the touch of his hand to mine had caused my heart to race.

I must be careful; I can see myself falling for someone like Matt and this cannot happen. I need to stay on track to reach the goals I have set for myself in my life. I have worked too hard not to become a Sports reporter.

I doze back off, dreaming of a life with Matt and what it would entail.

I wake, feeling refreshed and ready to take on the week, then spend the first few hours of the day on my interview with Matt. After hitting send, I feel like I have just turned in a best-selling novel to a publisher.

By the time I leave for work at Club E, I hadn't yet heard anything about my article. I arrive at the club and get changed for my first client.

My phone dings in my pocket. My editor tells me my interview with Matt will run in tomorrow's paper. He was pleased to hear that I have an appointment with Oratorio Salvador at the end of the week.

I knock on Ms. Sally's door and ask if she has a moment to speak with me.

"What's going on, Sable?"

"I turned in my interview with Matt Jones, and I have another interview Friday with his opponent."

"That's wonderful, everything you have worked so

hard for is finally happening. I'm so proud of you. You've worked so hard to make your dreams come true." She opens her arms wide, and I get up and step into her embrace.

"Thank you for everything, Sally. I love you." I wipe my eyes. "I'll see you in a couple of days for my next shift."

"I love you. Now get out of here before I get all blubbery." She dabs at her eyes with a tissue.

"Bye." I walk out the door and head to my car.

When I walk out the door, my phone dings; I have a text from Oratorio.

ORATORIO:

> I'm getting in to town later Friday than I thought. Meet me at the restaurant at eight p.m.?

ME:

> I'll see you there.

After, I changed into yoga pants and chilled the rest of the day. I send a quick text to Matt to see how his week has been. I know he's been busy training, but it's been a few days since I've seen him. I wish I could talk to Matt and be straight with him about everything.

My phone rings, and it's Matt calling. "Hi Matt," I answer.

"Hi, I was thinking of you when your text came through."

"You were? What were you thinking?" he asks.

"I need to hurry up and get back to town because I'm missing you. Besides, you promised me a redo on the dinner."

I can hear many people and buzzers or alarms going off in the background. "Where are you calling from?" I ask him.

"I'm in Vegas. We come up here to do some specialized training and to have a little fun before I begin my routine before for the fight. I'll be back in town Friday. Would you like to have dinner with me?"

"I have my interview with Oratorio Friday night. Otherwise, I would love to have dinner with you. What about Saturday?" I suggest.

"Saturday will work but let's make a day of it instead of just dinner. Dress casually and bring a swimsuit. He says to me. I'll have a car pick you up around eleven."

"Sounds like fun."

"See you Saturday, Sable."

I got a call from Ms. Sally informing me I had a client call and request a special session with me Friday at

3:00 p.m. When I asked her who it was, she had replied with, "It's not someone you're going to want to pass on."

My curiosity is piqued as I arrive at Club E around two to get ready for my client. I'm ready and waiting for their arrival as Ms. Sally knocks on my door.

"May I join you for a few minutes," she asks.

"Of course, are you going to tell me who my guest is?" I ask as I turn to look at the monitor I have pulled up on my laptop.

"It's Matt."

I jerk around to face her. "What? Matt?"

"Yes, he called and asked for a session with you. I tried to give him to someone else and he was adamant he only wanted to see you." She walks over and helps me braid my hair. "Sable, dear, does he know you're Madame E?"

"How can he?" I stammer. "I'm very careful. I don't wear the same cologne or use the same lotion. I even use a different shampoo and conditioner when I'm coming to work here Eddie has never been a client of mine." My heartbeat has picked up and my pulse races.

"Then there should be nothing to worry about." She finishes putting my hair up in a bun on my head. "He's here." Ms. Sally points at the monitor. "I'll go meet him. You take a moment and then I'll bring him back to you."

"Thank you." I turn to watch Matt greet Ms. Sally as she walks up. She stalls for me.

I quickly put the laptop away and sit on the end of the bed. There is a knock on the door. "Enter," I reply.

"Matt, how nice of you to come back and see me again." I prowl over to him allowing my gloved hand to slowly slide up his arm and across his broad muscular shoulders.

"So, what are you wanting to do today, Matt?" I run my hand up his neck, fisting his hair and pulling his head backward.

"I want to talk more about learning how to submit to be a better dom," he confesses.

"Why do you want to know how to be a better dom?" I push.

"What do you do outside of working here?" Matt asks. "You smell like orange blossoms. I love that smell."

"I didn't give you permission to ask questions, did I? You need to strip and kneel with your palms up on your thighs."

"Can't we just discuss how it all works?"

"I'm not into giving classes." I walk over and open the door. "Find yourself a teacher somewhere else."

"Maybe I will," he replies, inhaling deeply. "I do love the smell of orange blossoms." He winks and struts out the door.

I release a breath I didn't know I was holding. I walk over and get my laptop out of the drawer, set it on the dresser, and pull up the security footage. I see Matt talking with Ms. Sally. He leans in to give her a kiss on her cheek before leaving.

Ms. Sally heads my way. I'm not surprised when I hear my door open. "Are you all right, Sable?"

"Of course. Why? Did he say something to make you think otherwise?"

"No, just the opposite. He said he enjoyed his time with you and would most definitely be back."

"I'm so confused by him."

"Are you sure he doesn't suspect who you are?" Sally pushes.

"I'm seeing him tomorrow. I'll let you know after that." I undo my hair and shake it loose from the braid. "I have to get ready to go do my interview with Oratorio."

"All right, dear, you call me if you need anything." She squeezes my shoulder before leaving my room.

I go home shower and change, making sure to use my vanilla scented shampoo and lotion as I always do before going out anywhere.

I walk into Andrea's Restaurant and give the hostess my name. She tells me I'm the first to arrive, which makes me happy. I hate to have someone waiting on me.

Pulling out my compact, I do a last check on my makeup and lipstick. The waiter comes by, and I order a glass of wine while I wait. I have my notes out, and I'm going over them when I glance at my watch, realizing Oratorio is fifteen minutes late.

I pull my phone out of my purse to see if I have missed a call or text from him or his publicist. There is nothing.

"Fuck," I say to no one in particular. "Fu—"

"I hope you will accept my apology. I'm not in the habit of standing up a beautiful woman," someone cuts me off.

In front of me is a man I can only describe as a Greek god. Dark hair, dark eyes, and an olive complexion. He wears a white shirt, unbuttoned more than most men in California are comfortable with, but on him, it's perfect. His muscular build is not hidden but enhanced by his clothing.

"Oratorio, please take a seat." I motion my hand to the seat across from me. "I hope you didn't have any trouble finding the restaurant."

"No, your directions were perfect. My driver wasn't used to the traffic, though."

"I have lived in L.A. my entire life, and I'm still not used to the traffic," I say, then laugh.

The waiter comes, and Oratorio orders a bottle of the wine I'm drinking. We order food on his next visit to our table.

"Thank you for agreeing to the interview. I appreciate it."

"I would never turn down an evening with such a beautiful woman." As he reaches for his glass of wine, his eyes lower to my chest and raise back to my face. "Tell me, Sable, are you single?"

"I am." My face warms as he watches me intensely, so I change the subject and ask him questions for the interview.

This is not a date, I remind myself. *Maybe having interviews with athletes over dinner is something I have to rethink in my career.*

"Let's make a deal: you ask me a question, then I'll ask you one?" Oratorio suggests.

"Okay, what is your heritage? Your name is so unique," I ask him.

"My mother is Greek, and my father is Italian."

Our food arrives before he asks me his next question. I take a bite of mine. "Delicious."

"Tell me about your family," he asks.

That's a popular question. I shovel some food in my mouth as I ponder on how to circumvent the sad details of my childhood. For some reason, it was a lot easier to open up to Matt. "I have a best friend Gabby and a woman I look up to as a mother."

He shakes his head, passing me the turn.

"What is your family like?"

"I'm one of seven siblings. My father owns the gym where he and his four brothers learned to fight. My parents have been married for forty-nine years. We are a very close family. All my siblings and their families live in the same town we grew up in. Every Sunday, the entire family — including aunts, uncles, and cousins — gets together for dinner.

"I can't imagine growing up like that. Do you ever feel like escaping from having so many family members around all the time?"

"No, never; my family is everything to me." He takes a drink of his wine.

"When dating someone, does your family have to approve of her?"

Where the hell did that question come from? I think to myself. There's no way they would approve of Madame E.

"Of course, if my family doesn't like her, then it would never work."

"That is understandable since you are all so close," I reply.

We finish the rest of the questions and are having a

friendly conversation when my phone dings. "Excuse me." I pick it up to check the text.

GABBY:

Hey, when you get done, why don't you come by Dante's club? We're all here.

ME:

K.

"Is everything all right?" Oratorio asks, reaching over and touching my arm.

"My friend, the one I spoke about earlier?"

"Gabby?" he confirms.

I smile wide. "Yep, she invited me to meet them at the club tonight."

"Is there dancing at this club?" He leans forward over the desert, grinning and doing a little shimmy.

"Yes, do you like to dance?" I mimic the action.

"Sable, I'm Greek and Italian. We love to do anything that involves grinding and moving our hips," he says with a wicked grin, then waves for the waiter to come over. "Check, please."

ME:

I'm on my way.

I don't see any reason to mention to Gabby that I'm bringing a friend. *The more, the merrier* has always been our motto. I give my parking ticket to the waiter so he can have the valet pull my car around for me by the time I get outside.

Oratorio rides with me so he doesn't have to deal with his driver not knowing how to get there. He texts him the address and tells him where he will need to be picked up from later. Thank goodness my car is a convertible, or he would never have fit into it.

Seeing him look over the top of my windshield causes me to laugh.

seven

SABLE

W<small>E PULL IN FRONT OF THE CLUB</small>, <small>AND THE VALET TAKES MY</small> keys. People in line groan as we walk in instead of waiting in line. Dante meets me at the door, greeting me with a hug. "I'm so glad you could make it tonight, Sable. Who is your friend?"

"Dante, I would like you to meet Oratorio Salvador." Dante holds his hand out to shake hands with Oratorio, which he accepts.

"Welcome to my club. I'm honored to have you join us this evening, Mr. Salvador."

"Please call me Oratorio." He pats Dante on the shoulder.

"Dante, where is Gabby?" I ask, in order to bring him back from his star-struck state.

"Right this way." He takes my arm in his as he leads us back to the same table we were at on my birthday.

Gabby is on the dance floor as we arrive at the table. I set my bag down and prance out to join her. I hear a shrill squeal of delight as soon as she sees me. Then she notices who follows me on the dance floor, and I'm forgotten as Oratorio is surrounded.

Gabby takes my arm, whispering in my ear, "Damn, that is a Greek God if I've ever seen one."

"I know, and he's half Italian." I can't help but grin.

"We need to take an international vacation, my friend. If they make men like this." She looks at Oratorio as if he was fashioned by her favorite designer. "Are you going to take him for a ride tonight?"

"His family has to approve of anyone he dates. There is no way they would approve of me."

"I'm asking if you're going to fuck him, not marry him, Sable... Damn, I should be a sports reporter. Being dined by some of the sexiest men on earth sounds like the best job ever."

"At the moment, I'm not going to do either, Gabs. I'm here to dance." I can't help laughing as she shakes her head and dances with me. Gabby's statement stings more than I'm willing to admit.

Oratorio Dances with Gabby and me. The man can dance. He kept up with the two of us without a problem. We had all been taking our turns dancing with Oratorio when he wrapped his arms around my waist, pulling me back to him and grinding against my ass. I reach my arms up over my head, wrapping them around his neck.

My eyes close as we dance. Gabby says my name, and when I open my eyes, I see Matt coming across the dance floor directly at me.

"Take your hands off her!" Matt demands, his hands clenched into a fist and the same deadly look he gets when he's in the ring on his face.

Oratorio instead grips my hips tighter. "Ouch," I say, trying to get free of him. I turn to look at him. "Let me go." I jerk free, pissed these two grown-ass men are acting like cavemen at the moment. I just want to get away from both of them.

I can't believe this shit. I'm having a perfectly fun evening dancing and then Matt and Oratorio turn into cavemen ruining my evening.

"I don't think so, Sable; you came with me, that means you're leaving with me."

I jerk free of him. "I didn't come with you, dumbass. You. Rode. With. Me." I enunciate every word. "No one tells me what I'm going to do or whom I'm going home with but me."

Oratorio reaches for me, but Matt steps in front of me. "You heard her. It's time for you to leave."

I brush my hair off my shoulders where I'm sticky from sweating and dancing. I'm thinking this is going to end with Matt telling him to leave. I couldn't have been more wrong.

"Whatever," Oratorio says as he turns to leave but stops. "I'll see you in the ring, Matt. The winner gets Sable for the night."

My head snaps around to face Oratorio not believing what I just heard. "What the fuck did you say?" I run toward him. "You son of a bitch." I dodge Matt's arm as he tries to grab me as I push past him.

"You would be a feisty one in bed," he says, just as I slap him across the face.

I realize what I have done as I hear everyone in the club gasp at the same time. Reality of the tonight's events and what the fall out means for my future hits me.

A strong arm comes around my waist, lifting my feet off the floor; I'm kicking and cussing to be released.

"A real man doesn't bet using a woman; they are not a possession. What I will do is promise to kick your ass and take your title from you. Get the fuck out of here before we find out tonight who is better," Matt tells him while holding me in his arms.

"We shall see, Jones."

Dante walks up with a couple of his security guards. "It's time for you to leave, Oratorio... We have called a car, and it is outside waiting on you."

"Matt, you can put me down." I wiggle in his arms, trying to get free.

He replies, "I think we need to discuss why you were here with Oratorio first."

"Excuse me?" I turn to face him when he finally puts me down.

"Why did you bring him here?" Matt asks.

"Let's go sit down." I take his hand and walk up to our table. Matt sits next to me. "Matt, I don't understand why this is so important to you. I appreciate you stepping in, but... Matt, we aren't together. I had a great time with you at dinner, and I think we could become excellent friends."

"Sable, I didn't say I wanted to spend the rest of my life with you; I asked you why you brought him here?" Matt sits back in his seat. I can see his fighter persona coming out.

"You're right: you didn't. I brought him here because he is a sexy man whom I had been having a nice time with. He was new to town. Since he didn't know anyone, I was being nice." I take a drink from the glass of wine the waitress handed me. Bravery, ego, or just plain spite kicked in at that moment. "That's a bunch of bullshit. He looked like a damn Greek God, and I was hoping I would take him home and fuck all night." I downed the rest of my wine, standing and walking back to the dance floor, not bothering to turn around and look at Matt.

Gabby dances up to me. "You good?"

"I'm great. Let's drink and dance the night away."

Gabby flags down Dante and signals to him that we need shots. Lots of shots. He meets us back at our table. Matt is not here when we walk up, so I look around to see if I see him.

"He left," Dante tells me.

"Oh..." is all I can manage to get out. I pick up the shot of tequila and down it.

Dante fills the shot glasses again. I down another. "Do we need some hors d'oeuvres?" Dante asks, and I ignore him.

Gabby must have answered Dante because an assortment of deliciousness arrives a few minutes later. I keep drinking shots and dancing. Gabby keeps trying to feed me food, but I don't eat.

We stay and close down the club. Gabby and Dante bring me home in my car. Only a real best friend passes up getting laid to stay the night and hold my hair as I puke my soul up in between lying on the cool bathroom floor tile.

I wake up on the floor of the master bathroom. I try to sit up, but my head feels like it will explode. I hear someone moving around in my bedroom and slowly pull myself up on the toilet. I don't remember anything about last night.

Why the hell am I on the floor? I think to myself.

"Hello?" I whisper, grabbing my head.

A second later, Gabby opens the door. "Hi, yourself; I'm glad you're awake. Here, take these." She holds her hand out with two white oblong pills with the word *acetaminophen* stamped on them. "Now drink this." A steaming cup of black coffee is placed in my hands. "I'll be right back." She leaves the bathroom. I can hear her in my bedroom, but I'm unsure what she is doing.

She comes back carrying some clothes. "You stink of alcohol and puke. Shower and put these on. I'll be in the living room. Do you need help, or can you stand alone?"

"I'm fine, Gabs. I got this." I take another sip of my coffee, then stand. I put down my mug and bend over to start the water for the shower. After undressing, I get in and stand under the warm water. I turn the hot water up higher. After a few minutes, my body reacts to the water's heat.

I finish with my shower and wrap my hair in a towel. Once I'm done drying off, I pull on the shorts and T-shirt Gabby had brought in, then walk into the living room, where I overhear Gabby speaking to someone. "She's fine. She's in the shower. I'll tell her you called. Bye, Matt."

"What was that all about?" I ask her, then refill my coffee cup.

"Matt was worried about you after last night."

"Why? It's not like he has any claim on me. It's none of his business who I fuck or how much I am fucking drinking. Plus, he was gone when I started to drink."

At least I remember that part.

"Why... What the fuck, Sable? He was concerned. He's a decent guy." She starts gathering up her stuff to leave.

"Where are you going?"

"I'll come back when the bitch with the hangover is gone, and my friend is back." Gabby walks out the door, slamming it behind her.

"Fuck." I flop down on the couch and finish my second cup of coffee. She's right: I am being a bitch. I have no reason to be mad at Matt or angry toward Gabby, so I text her.

ME:

> I'm sorry. You didn't deserve any of that. Thanks for staying and taking care of me. Your sober, over-being-a-bitch friend.

Dante is my following text.

ME:

Good morning... I wanted you to know I appreciate you bringing me home with Gabby last night. I'm sorry if I did anything to embarrass you or your club. I will completely understand if I need to stay away for a while. Just know I don't usually act that way.

My following text will take me some time to decide what to say. *Maybe I should bite the bullet and call him?* I sit there and try to remember everything I had said to Matt. The last thing I remember is him picking me up and holding me to keep me from going after Oratorio.

Oh, to hell with it. I pull up his name and push call. The phone begins to ring, and he picks it up right away.

"Sable?"

"Hi, Matt." I take a deep breath to continue. "Thank you for stepping in and stopping me from making a fool out of myself last night."

"You weren't making a fool out of yourself. You were pissed, and I was afraid you would break your hand by hitting him." Matt laughs into the phone.

I chuckle. "With my luck, I would have." I take a moment. "Seriously, thank you, and thanks for checking on me."

"Have you eaten anything yet?" Matt asks.

"No."

"What if I pick you up and we go to breakfast?"

"Okay." I give him my address. "I'll see you soon." I hurry to the bathroom and put on some mascara and lip gloss. There is no way I'm going to attempt to hide the puffiness of my eyes. I don't bother to put my hair up. I just brush it and put on some tennis shoes.

The doorbell rings; I look at my phone and see it's Matt at the door.

After grabbing my purse, I open my door. "I'm all set."

"You look great compared to what I described this morning." Matt chuckles.

"Thanks, I think," I respond as I follow him to his Camaro.

"This car is amazing. Is it 1968?"

"I'm impressed, and yes, it is. How did you learn about cars?" Matt asks, pulling into a diner not far from my house.

"Wait... How do you know this place?" I point out the window. "I eat here all the time. I live right around the corner."

"We live in the same neighborhood?" Stepping out of the car, I take a good look at Matt. All these years, I had never run into him anywhere. I would have remembered that.

I can't believe what I'm hearing.

"I live behind you," he locks the doors and gestures toward the building. "I realized it last night when I followed Dante and Gabby as they brought you home." We step inside and are immediately met with the scent of apple pie. The scent of cinnamon and bread fills the air. At that moment my stomach begins to growl.

"Why did you follow them to my home?" I ask, starting to freak out.

"Relax, Sable; I picked Dante up and took him home. That's why your car was at your house."

My shoulders relax, and so does my breathing. "Sorry, living alone all these years has taught me to be careful of my privacy and security."

"That makes sense. There are some crazies out there. Have you ever thought about getting a dog or a gun?" He takes a drink of the coffee the waitress brought us, and she takes our order.

"I work too much to have a dog and give it the attention it needs. A gun isn't something I want to have on me. I know how to protect myself if I need to," I assure him.

Matt drinks his coffee and looks at me over the edge of the mug. "After last night, I'm curious as to how you would protect yourself."

"I have taken quite a few self-defense classes and a few martial-arts classes. I hold a black belt in Karate and a red belt in Taekwondo." I take a drink of my coffee. "I found out when I was living at home that I needed to be able to protect myself from my mom's male friends."

"Sable, I will say, you are not like any woman I have ever met." His smile reaches his eyes, causing them to sparkle.

"Is that a good thing?" I ask him.

"That's an excellent thing, as far as I'm concerned. You punched a World Champion MMA fighter without any hesitation. That's badass," he responds excitedly.

"Not sure my boss would see it that way."

"A story is a story, right?" he says with a smile. "As long as I'm still your big break, I promise not to get jealous."

"I'm just lucky my boss hasn't found out yet. Interviewing an athlete normally doesn't mean dinner, dancing, and an out-of-the-ring knock-out session." Not that I knocked him out, but it could have gotten out of hand with Matt and him.

"You haven't been on the internet today, have you?"

"No, why?"

"Eddie sent me this first thing this morning. It's another reason I came by to see you today." He hands me his phone, and there is a video of me punching Oratorio, and then another of Matt hoisting me onto his shoulder and carrying me like a massive bag of dog food.

"There goes my career." I put my face in my hands.

"What the fuck is wrong with me? I was so close to getting the career of my dreams." I wipe a loose tear with a napkin Matt hands me.

"Nobody said this is going to affect your career. Hell, it's liable to help it." He tries to encourage me.

"How? I'm now a laughingstock."

"Your video was viewed by a lot of people. Your subscribers have increased to over fifty thousand. I think that can make you an asset."

What? Well, fifty thousand is not that much... but it's something to think about.

The waitress delivers our food. Neither of us says anything for a few minutes. Me, mostly digesting the shitload of information just dropped on me. Maybe Matt has a point, but my gut is telling me otherwise.

"You ok—" Matt's cut off by my phone going off.

"Speak of the devil..." I murmur as I check the message my editor just sent. "I'm about to find out how bad it will get. I have to be at the television station this afternoon."

Matt doesn't say anything, he just keeps eating. After a few minutes, he picks up his phone and sends a text, still not saying anything to me.

"Is everything all right?" I ask him.

"Sorry, I have a habit of getting an idea and running with it and forgetting to talk to others about it."

"So, what is your idea?" I see him shift his eyes from me to behind me. He breaks into a smile.

"Why don't you come over and sit beside me?" He stands, and I slide into the booth. He hands my food and coffee to me. After another thirty minutes, I see what, rather who, his idea is as Eddie and Gabby come walking toward us.

Had they been together?

"Good morning; thank you guys for coming." Matt shakes Eddie's hand and gives Gabby a hug and kiss on her cheek.

"You said it was important," Gabby responds. "How are you feeling?" She looks at me.

I shrug. "Like a terrible friend."

"You should." She smiles and takes my hand. "Luckily, I'm a better friend than you and I will forgive you."

"I love you, Gabs."

"Is this what you called us here for?" Eddie asks, looking confused.

"No." Matt shows him the internet video with over a million views.

"Holy shit, Sable, you have a hell of a right cross." He chuckles.

Gabby looks at me. "Has the station seen this?"

I just nod my head. "I have a meeting with them this afternoon. Matt thinks it could be good for me, but..." I can't even bring myself to finish the thought.

"Don't worry." Gabby points to my plate. "Hurry up and finish eating. I have an idea. I don't think we should discuss it here."

Matt and I finish eating.

"Should we go back to my house?" I ask Gabby.

As Matt pays for our breakfast, I pull Gabby to the side. "I'm sorry about the way I acted."

"I know that." She texts feverishly. "Okay, we are set; let's get to your house." She climbs into Eddie's car with him, and I get in the car with Matt. *Hmm. They came in one car.*

"Do you have any idea what she is up to," he asks me.

Other than getting involved with Eddie and Dante? "No, but I trust her."

eight

SABLE

We pull up at my house, and the four of us are met by Oratorio and his publicist.

"Let's hurry up and get inside," Gabby says, leading everyone in. "Have a seat, everyone... Oratorio, thank you for coming and trying to help Sable out," she tells him.

Being in the same room with Oratorio makes my anger resurface. To think he wanted to use me as a prize in a bet. It's taking everything I have to remain sitting here and not jump up to kick him in the head.

"It was a great evening out. I took it too far. That's why we are here. Gabby reached out and told us what was going on. We want to help," Oratorio replies, looking at me. "I'm terribly sorry, Sable."

Eddie speaks up, "Gabby, what's your plan? Sable has to be at the station in only a few hours."

"What if Matt does a video saying he's never had women protect his honor until last night when Sable punched Oratorio for saying he would kick his ass?"

"That will never work. What about my interview with Oratorio?" I finally speak up.

"You use the video as a follow-up. Tell the truth; you were out with everyone and were having a great time until Matt showed up. No offense, Matt." She looks at him shrugging her shoulders.

"None taken."

Yes, but what does that say about my credibility as a reporter. I don't want to be known as the anchor who sleeps with her interviewees. That's almost as bad as being outed for being Madame E. I think to myself.

Gabby continues, "The two men started going back and forth about the upcoming fight, and Oratorio bragged about winning the fight easily. Insults were thrown, and you let your emotions get the better of you... and you hit him." Gabby mimics the punch, using one of her palms to represent Oratorio's face. I wince at the smacking sound.

"I don't like it," Matt and Eddie say simultaneously.

"The station will see Sable as unpredictable and a liability."

"Why not just tell them the truth?" I suggest.

"I agree," Oratorio chimes in. "We were dancing; Matt came in, and we started arguing. I threw out the idea of the bet — the winner gets Sable — and she decks me. Matt grabs her to keep her from breaking something."

"You would be okay with that?" I ask him, my shoulders squaring as my back stiffens as I prepare for his response.

"It's the truth. I honestly deserved it. I was pushing Matt and using you to do it." His eyes divert to the floor. "It was a dick move, and I apologize for it. Sable, tell the studio the truth. I'll back you if I'm asked any questions." Oratorio leans back, sprawling his arms over the back of my couch.

"Do you want me to pull the interview?" I ask him.

"No, it was a good interview. It was nice to actually talk about my family and not just quote stats through the whole thing. Hell, women are going to love the idea that I would fight for a night in bed with them. I'll get even more pussy than before." He looks at me with a grin. "We are going to go, Sable. Let me know if you need anything else." He turns to Matt. "I'll see you in the ring." The two shake hands, and Gabby walks them to the door.

I open my laptop on the counter and pull up the video. It now has over two million views. Everyone is asking who I am.

Hopefully, a reporter after this, I answer as I scroll through the comments.

After, Matt and Gabby let themselves out, and I promise to let them know how it goes at the station.

I finish writing Oratorio's interview and submit it to the station, just in case the truth still gets me fired. I then write a rebuttal to all the viewers of the video.

I'm Sable, a freelance writer and the woman in this video with Oratorio Salvador and Matt Jones. I had previously interviewed Matt Jones about his upcoming fight against Oratorio Salvador for the World Championship Title.

On the night of this video, I had an interview with Oratorio Salvador to get his perspective. He and I wound up at the same club. We were on the dance floor when Matt Jones came in.

The two men started arguing about the upcoming fight; It came down to a whose-penis-is-bigger competition. I was going to walk away, and Oratorio threw out the idea that there should be a bet, and I should be the prize for the evening. The thought of a man suggesting something like this about me or any other woman infuriated me, so I punched him.

I know, stupid move. My hand hurts like hell.

I really didn't think Oratorio meant what he said. During our interview, he seemed to really care about his family and he's very passionate about his career. I think the idea of seeing his opponent outside of the ring got his emotions and ego going.

The next video of Matt carrying me out like a caveman is well...

I think about this before continuing. *Should I be honest?* They both said to be, what do I have to lose? *I was a little tipsy, and I don't mind admitting I have had a massive crush on Matt Jones for a long time. He drove me home to make sure I arrived safely. That is the truth about the videos and what happened at the club.*

Thank you all for listening to my side of the story.

Bye,

Sable

I push publish, and it goes live. I'm amazed watching the number of views keep climbing. My video goes viral for a second time. My numbers climb into the millions.

As I walk into the studio, I'm greeted by the receptionist and am led toward Mr. Marty Mathews, head of SportsTV Network.

"Sable, please come in." Marty Mathews is not what I expect for a head of a Sports Network. He is a man of small stature. He and I are possibly the same size if I'm barefoot. He is balding and casually dressed in khakis and a white polo shirt.

"Thank you." I slide past him into a conference room.

I am shocked to see Matt, Oratorio, and Sam Thomas, the editor I had been talking with, all in the room.

"Hello, everyone," I nervously say.

"Please take a seat." Mr. Mathews points toward a chair next to Matt.

"Sable, we are all here because of your interviews with these two athletes and the video that has come to light. Until this morning, we were prepared to offer you a position."

I take a deep breath and try to hold back the tears threatening to fall at his words. *Prepared.* I'm done; everything I had worked so hard for is now over.

Matt reaches under the table and takes my hand in his. I am not saying a word, just holding his hand and gently squeezing it. I have to admit I'm terrified.

"What have you decided?" I ask, not able to wait any longer.

"Honestly after having the video brought to my attention there was no way I was going to hire you. That is, until you explained what happened. Your direct approach shows you can be trusted to bring the truth to the people. You're someone who will treat the athletes fairly but not be afraid to make the hard choices when it comes to telling the truth. We would like to offer you a position as a sportscaster here at Channel FZWA 105."

Oratorio and Matt both yell, "Hell yeah!"

I respond, "Now I don't know what to say, except I accept. Thank you." I stand and shake the studio official's hand.

"Temporary, of course. We want to get a feel for your work. Why don't you come in Monday at eight a.m., and we will get all your paperwork taken care of along with the grand tour?"

"That sounds great. Thank you again for giving me this opportunity."

"Oh, and Sable..." Mr. Mathews says. "No punching anyone else." He laughs.

"Yes, sir, not unless they need it." I wink at him.

Matt, Oratorio, and I walk out the door and to the parking lot. "What are the two of you doing here?"

"We caused this, so we wanted to be here to help clean it up. Congratulations on the new job." Oratorio hugs me. He struts off and gets in his car.

"Want to celebrate?" Matt asks.

"What did you have in mind?" I ask, leaning against my car.

He steps closer to me. "I don't know; we could grab a pizza and go to your place and watch something on TV."

"That sounds perfect to me."

"It does?"

"Yes, why do you want to go out?" I look at him.

"No, I'm just surprised that you agreed to stay in. I figured you always liked going out on the town."

I couldn't help but laugh. After I quit laughing, I tell Matt. "I'm a homebody. Gabby usually drags me out of the house kicking and screaming."

"You are full of surprises, Sable. Let's go to your house, or do you want to go to mine?"

"Mine is closer," I joke. "Do you have your car here?"

"I do; I'll follow you home." He leans in and gives me a soft kiss on my lips. "I have a crush on you as well."

I open my mouth and watch him walk off toward his car. Matt just kissed me. I smile to myself as I realize he watched my video.

"What do you like on your pizza?" Matt asks, resting against my counter.

"Well, that's a loaded question for two people getting to know each other. Pizza has very personal preferences, such as white or red sauce, thick or thin. Anchovies or none," I tease him.

"I have an idea," Matt suggests. "I'll go in the other room and order my favorite pizza, and you stay here and order yours."

"That's a great idea. Test our compatibility?" I wink at him as he saunters out of my kitchen. "By the way, if you order anchovies, it's a hard limit!" I shout toward the living room to test if he can hear me, then hit Joe's Pizza on my phone. "Hi Joe, it's Sable; I'll take my regular and extra garlic bread, perfect. Thank you." I open the fridge to see what I have to drink.

Matt comes in. "You all done?"

"Sure, I am. It'll be here in twenty minutes. Would you like wine, beer, or a soft drink?"

"A beer, please."

I grab a beer from the fridge and hand it to him, then grab myself a soft drink. I get some paper plates and napkins out of the cabinet. We small talk about fighters and stats, and before we know it, the doorbell rings.

Matt says, "That's the pizzas! I'll get them."

The door opens, and I hear Matt, "Hi Joe, thanks for delivering the pizzas." Matt comes back into the house.

I have brought the drinks and plates into the living room so we can watch TV as we eat.

He hands me the pizza with his name on it. "We open them on three. One, two, three."

We both open our pizza boxes and start laughing. They are the same: alfredo sauce, Italian sausage, spinach, mushroom, black olives, and pepper flakes, and both are on a hand-tossed crust.

"You have to be kidding. You order the same pizza as I do?" I ask, then take a bite.

Matt takes a bite of his piece. "All this time, we have lived around the corner from each other, getting the same pizza, and we have never met."

"True." I smile and grab the TV remote. "Do you mind if we watch the fights tonight?" I flip the TV to sports pay-per-view. "The Women's Championship Fight is on."

"You must have some hidden flaws because I only see perfection." Matt pulls me in his arms and kisses me intensely. His hand goes to the back of my head fisting my hair.

I push my chest against him. "Giving back as good as I'm getting." The tension between us is electrifying. We part lips both of us breathless. "Wow" I whisper as he never breaks eye contact with me. I'm really glad we didn't sleep together at Club E. I want our first time to be together with out any masks as ourselves.

"Wow, is right."

nine

I SIT BACK, PUTTING MY ARM OVER THE SPINE OF THE SOFA behind Sable. She curls into my side. I never thought I would find a woman that liked to watch fights as much as I do. She is gorgeous, sexy as sin, intelligent, and loves sports.

What are her flaws? I think to myself.

My thumb slowly rubs the bare skin of her arm. I'm not paying attention to the fight on TV. I bring Sable closer, putting my fingers under her chin and lifting her face toward mine. I lean down and kiss her.

She pushes me down to lie back on the couch, her body covering mine. I let her take the lead regarding how fast and far she wanted this to go tonight. My mind goes back to Madame E. Let's see how demanding Sable can be.

Sable pushes my shirt up; I raise my shoulders,

allowing her to pull it over my head. She kisses and nips with her teeth all down my chest until she reaches my nipples. She sucks one into her mouth and uses her teeth to scrape along the tender skin before sucking it again. It's as if my nipple suddenly has a direct path to my cock.

Sable moans as she wiggles, feeling my stiff cock under her body. She raises to a sitting position and takes her shirt off. To my surprise, she doesn't have a bra underneath, only a thin lace tank top. I rub the palm of my hand across her rigid nipple, causing her to moan loudly.

I undo the button and zipper of her pants. "Sable, we will have to go to the bedroom or get on the floor. This couch isn't big enough for the two of us."

She laughs and stands, holding her hand out to me. I sit up, taking her hand and letting her lead me to her bedroom. She closes the door as soon as we enter. When she turns the light on, I'm surprised to see the blood-red bedding on the four-post bed. Even more surprised to see the gold rings on each bedpost.

I walk over, running my hand over the post and ring. "This is interesting," I tell her.

She walks into my arms. "Those are for another time. Tonight is about getting to know each other." She gets on her tiptoes and brushes her lips against mine while she undoes my jeans, sliding her hand along the inside of the waistband. Her soft fingers smooth along my skin as she works her way down and slowly takes my jeans with her hands.

I lift her in my arms; her legs wrap around my waist. I can feel the heat from her core through her jeans. I walk up to the mattress and gently lie her down, pulling her pants off her long, beautiful legs.

I kick off my jeans and slowly climb up her body, leaving kisses and nips along her skin as I make my way to the sweetness that awaits me. Sable's eyes don't close. They watch every move I make. Her tongue comes out long enough to moisten her lips before disappearing back into her mouth.

I take a moment to admire her perfectly manicured pubic area, then place kisses along her lips. She tries to open her legs, but I hold them in place. Slowly, I slide my tongue along the slit, and a delicious moan escapes Sable.

Grabbing her knees, I spread them apart and dive into her heat. She is so wet and ready, and I lap along her core until I feel her begin to quiver. "Give it to me, Sable. Give me all of it." I suck on her taunt nub until a scream escapes her as her body convulses with her release.

She tries to pull me up her body, "Not yet, baby, you need to give me one more." I slowly lap at her sensitive clit. Her body jumps when I gently touch it and suck it into my mouth, flicking my tongue over it. I slide three fingers inside her as I nip her clit with my teeth. I pound my fingers in and out of her, going faster and harder with each thrust.

Sable comes undone with no warning. Her core clenches my fingers, trying to pull them deeper inside as her juices flow freely from her body.

I slowly crawl up her body, kissing her skin as I go. I spread her legs apart, and she wraps her legs around my waist. I waste no time as I ram my rock-hard cock into her body.

Sable raises her hips, matching me pound for pound. I roll us both over, putting her on top of my body. She raises her knees and rides me as if I'm a bucking bull. She throws her head back, rolling one of her nipples between her fingers as she holds onto my hand with her other.

Gawd, she is beautiful when she comes undone.

I grab her hips and help her keep the momentum as my release comes. She lays forward on top of my body. I wrap my arms around her as she puts her head on my chest.

"I'll be right back. I enter the bathroom running the water until it is warm. I return to the bedroom with the warm cloth and begin to care for Sable. I wash her carefully to ensure she will not be too sore later." I crawl back in bed with her, and she climbs back to lie on my body.

"If you need to take off, I understand." She starts to roll off me.

"No, I told you... I feel different when I'm with you. I want to stay the night if you're all right with it."

She crosses her arms on my chest and rests her chin on them. "I haven't had a man spend the night in my home in a very long time. I like the idea of spending the night in your arms." She leans up to kiss me.

"Do you have any plans tomorrow?" I ask her.

"No, why?"

"Just checking... because I don't see either of us getting much sleep tonight."

"Sleep is overrated." She begins to kiss me deeply.

My cock is hard and ready to go again. "Get on your knees," I tell her. Without hesitation, she does as she is told. I rub my cock, coating it in her juices before slamming it into her core.

When we both release, we collapse on our sides. With my arm draped over her waist, I hold her against me. I know when she falls asleep because her breathing becomes shallow. The air conditioner kicks on, and she snuggles against me, trying to stay warm. I pull up a sheet to cover us both. Sable releases a soft moan and kisses my chest before returning to sleep.

I lie awake, looking at this beautiful, sexy woman in

my arms, wondering what makes me want to be so careful with her. I've always wanted to make a woman submit, to do as I command and have no say in bed. Yet tonight was about pleasing Sable; I was completely turned on and satisfied by doing that.

I fall asleep with these thoughts and this amazing woman in my arms.

During the night, I wake to find Sable sucking my cock. I look down at her, and she stops long enough to smile and say, "I had gotten hungry, and here you were."

I don't think I've ever had a blow job like this. I swear she's going to suck my balls out of my cock.

Sable curls into my side, "Let's sleep a little longer."

I wrap her in my arms, kissing her on her forehead. We both fall asleep.

A few hours later, I wake to the smell of coffee. Rolling over, I find an empty bed. I go into the bathroom and come out, then put on my boxers to search for Sable and coffee.

Walking into the kitchen, I see her bent over, looking inside the fridge... wearing my T-shirt. I come up behind her, wrapping my arms around her waist, and pull her back against me.

"Mmm." She wiggles against me and leans against my chest.

I move her hair to the side and kiss her neck. "Would you like me to cook breakfast?"

"You cook?"

"I do."

"What if we cook together?" She turns in my arms to face me.

"I would love to cook with you, baby; I'll do whatever you want to do together." I pull her in and kiss her.

"Oh, that's a big statement."

"I mean it. Why didn't I find you before I have to start my grueling training schedule tomorrow?" I push some hair behind her ear.

"Are you saying you won't have time for me during your training?" She looks disappointed. Trying to hide it she begins to pull items out of the refrigerator.

I try to reassure her. "I'm saying we will have to figure out a schedule that works for both of us; I want to try it if you do."

"I would like to try and see where this goes. I know that your training comes first. I get that." She begins to crack eggs in a bowl after she hands me bacon to begin to cook. "What does your training schedule consist of?"

"I'm up at five a.m. and run ten miles. I spend four hours working out then another two hours sparing. I promise to do everything I can to make time for us." She hugs me. "There's one other thing. "What's that?"

"I'm celibate when I'm training for a fight. It keeps me focused."

"Let's cook." She doesn't respond.

"Sable, did you hear what I said?" I place my hands on her hips, turning her to face me.

"I heard you. We will just do other things."

"Really?"

"I'm going to miss the sex, but I still want to spend time with you. You need to focus on the fight. It's too important for your career. I want you to do everything you can to win. I don't want you to get hurt." She wraps her arms around my waist.

"I won't get hurt." I tuck a strand of hair behind her ear. "I'm hungry, what do we have?" I look in the fridge.

"Bacon, onion, peppers, cheese, eggs. I can make omelets."

"Okay, I'll make blueberry pancakes to go with them." We both set to cook our assigned items. I'm going to need to go for a run after eating all this food." She states. "You run?"

"Yes, do you find that hard to believe?" She laughs.

"No, I was thinking that is something we can do together."

"That's a great idea. We can go after eating."

We eat breakfast, then put the dishes in the dishwasher.

"What do you say we go for a run, then come back and take a shower? We can save water, and I can help you by washing your back and hair."

"Okay, let me go get changed." I start to follow her to the bedroom. "No, sir, you stay right here until I'm dressed, or we aren't ever going to get out of here."

"But..."

"I'll make it up to you later," she promises, walking off with extra sway in her hips.

"You're an evil little minx, aren't you?"

"Me?" She points at her chest. She laughs as she closes the door.

A few minutes later, she comes out in shorts, a T-shirt, hair in a ponytail, and tennis shoes. "Okay, stud, you can get dressed."

I throw on my jeans and T-shirt, which smells like Sable. I walk into the front room and see her sitting on the front porch on her phone.

"All ready, we just need to stop by my place so I can change." I sit beside her on the step.

She has a sad face. "Sable, what's going on?" "It's just Gabby; she thinks we are going too fast."

"Hey, if you want to slow things down at any time, let me know. But it has to be your decision, not Gabby's. I don't want to date her."

"You want to date me?"

"I want to get to know you; dating someone is how that is normally done. Don't give up on us until we have given ourselves a chance, okay?"

"Okay." She kisses me.

ten

MATT

I stand, taking her hand. "Let's go to my place so I can change."

We start walking to the corner and turn left. We go down three houses and are at the house behind Sable's. "This is it." Walking up to the door, I unlock it and step aside to let her in.

"Look around while I change." I go upstairs and slip on my running gear. I hear the back door open and look out the window. I see Sable in the backyard looking over the fence into her yard. I can see her laughing as she comes back into the house.

I'm walking down the stairs as she comes in. "You look like you're having a good time. What's so funny?"

"You can see straight into my backyard. I lay out there in the nude."

"I need to spend more time at home and less time at

the gym. I have been missing out. I would have made sure we met a long time ago if I had ever seen you lying outside naked."

"Here I was worried about the neighbors on the side, and you could've been peeping right through the bushes the whole time."

"I could have." I pull her to me. "You ready to go?"

She nods her head and strolls back into the house. After she slips her phone into the pocket of her shorts, we take off down the sidewalk, starting slow until we get warmed up. I get her to slow down as we enter the park. "I didn't ask you how far you usually go?"

"I do ten miles daily, five going and five back. What about you?" she says

"I do ten, then another ten on the gym treadmill."

"Let's get going." She takes off ahead of me.

We finish our run and stop back at my house. "Want to shower here, or would you prefer to do it at your house?"

"I can shower here if I can borrow a shirt and some shorts."

"You know we can go through the back gate to your house."

"I don't have a key for the gate. The old owners didn't leave it," she tells me.

"Let's go try something. I have these keys. Let's see if they work." We walk outside. There is a whole key ring full of keys. This one says gate, sticking the key in the lock on his side, the key turns, and the gate moans from years of not being open. With a final pull, I get the gate to open.

The vines that have grown through the gate need to be cleaned to allow for more effortless opening and closing, but for now, it will enable Sable to go into her home and get some clothes to wear.

"I'll run in, grab a change of clothes, and be back." She goes across her yard into her house.

Sable goes into the house and I pour myself some orange juice. A few minutes later, she walks in carrying a small duffel. "When I realized everything, I needed, I almost called and said I would take a shower at my house, but I seem to remember something about a backwash and my hair wash."

"Come on; I'll show you the bedroom to put your stuff in." We go upstairs to the master bedroom.

"Wow, this is nice. Your bed is huge. That's bigger than a California King, isn't it?" She slides her hand along the sled footboard. She feels the rings on the footboard like she has her own. She flips one of the black metal rings, so it clangs against the bed. Sable looks at me and does the same thing I did. "Interesting." She smirks and keeps walking, looking around.

Walking into the bathroom, I hear her say, "Oh my, I think I'm in heaven." I see her standing in the shower, looking around. There are six shower heads, and there is a jacuzzi tub as well, along with a double sink. "Matt, this room is beautiful."

"Thank you, I needed room to help me relax my sore muscles after working out and after matches." I walk up to her and help her lift her shirt over her head. I unhook her bra and helped her off with her shoes, socks, and shorts.

"My turn to unwrap my present," she says while helping me strip bare. I reach in, turn on the water, and adjust the temperature.

I step in, holding my hand out for Sable as she steps in with me. With the flip of a lever, the overhead rain shower heads come on. It's as if we are standing outside in our very own rainstorm. I flip another lever that shuts off, and a massage spout comes on. I dump some shampoo in my hair and begin to wash Sable's hair.

I turn the rain shower head on to rinse her hair. I put conditioner on her hair, directing her back to the shower corner, and have her sit down while I use a washcloth to lather her body. I take her hand to have her stand as I wash her back, and then use the hand-held shower head to rinse her hair and body. I have her sit back down as I begin to wash my hair.

I feel a soapy washcloth on my chest. I open my eyes to see Sable lathering my body. She makes sure every inch of me is touched and clean. She uses the same handheld shower head to rinse my body. When the washing is done, I shut the water off, grab a towel, and wrap it around Sable's body. I hand her another one for her hair.

I'm impressed. In a few seconds, she has her hair wrapped in the terry cloth and on top of her head in no time. My phone rings as we walk back into the bedroom. Eddie.

"Yes?" I pick it up. "No, man, I'm busy; I'll see you tomorrow at six a.m. at the gym. Talk to you later."

"Matt, do I need to go? I don't want to be stopping you from getting ready for your fight?" Sable asks, starting to open her bag to get her clothes out.

"Hey, I don't want you to leave. I was hoping you would stay and have dinner with me before I take you home. I have to be at the gym early, so it may be an early night."

She looks at the floor instead of me.

I raise her chin so I can see her eyes. "Do you want to spend the evening with me, Sable?"

"I would like that."

"Good, but first, I haven't finished my day's exercise." I tackle Sable onto the bed, knocking her bag of clothes to the floor. "You won't be needing those for a while."

She starts to speak, but I kiss her to take her mind

off the words she wants to say. Her hair falls loose from the towel, so I drop the towel to the floor.

"What kind of exercise is this?" Sable asks breathlessly.

"Cardio." I slide down her body, bending her knees to place her feet on the edge of the bed. This position opens her wide for me. I dive in, fucking her with my tongue.

Sable comes apart quickly; she tries to push her legs together to get me to stop my relentless oral attack.

I don't stop. The more she fights me, the faster I go.

I coax another orgasm from her before I release her legs. I left her limp body on the bed and crawl in beside her to snuggle. "Are you okay?"

She doesn't form any words, just nods her head yes.

"Do you want me to stop?"

"No, just give me a minute to catch up," she whispers into my chest.

"Why don't you roll over and let me give you a massage," I tell her.

"I should be doing it for you," she replies.

"I promise to call you after a hard day of training, and you can come over and give me a massage," I answer her.

"Okay."

I put some lotion on my hands and work on her

neck and shoulders. At my touch, the knots start to release.

Sable's moans go straight to my cock.

I add more lotion to do her lower back and massage her buttocks simultaneously. Her ass is firm and plump; I can't help leaning down to give it a kiss and a nip, causing her to moan deeper. I pull her up to her knees. I line my cock up to her core, coating it in all her juices.

Without taking it slow, I ram into her hard and unrelenting, over and over. She tries to get up on her hands, but I put my palm between her shoulder blades, pushing her down into the mattress.

Sable surprises me by begging for more. "Give it to me. I want it all."

I go harder.

"Come on, I know you got more."

Sable's words are the biggest fucking turning-on I've ever had. Never has a woman tried to tell me what she wants.

"Don't hold back, Matt. Give it to me."

That's it. I can't hold it any longer. I come deep inside her and smack her ass as I do.

That pushes Sable over the edge. She screams, "Yes!"

There is a lot Sable and I need to discuss regarding our sexual appetites. I can see we have similar tastes in some areas. With the championship fight coming up, I can't afford the time to explore them right now, but I will. I just have to find a way not to lose her in the meantime.

"Hey," she asks as I lie on my back, thinking. "What's wrong?"

"I was just thinking that I wish I had more time with you before I have to begin training." I roll onto my side to face her.

"Matt, I'm not going anywhere unless you tell me you're not interested, and then I'll walk away. We have a lot to discuss and discover about each other after this fight. But... first, you did promise me dinner, and I'm starving." She leans in and kisses me.

"Do you want to go out or call for takeout?"

"Let's go see what you have in your fridge." She grabs her clothes and quickly gets dressed. She goes downstairs ahead of me, opening the fridge and setting a rotisserie chicken on the counter with milk, parmesan cheese, heavy cream, and mushrooms. She opens and closes cabinets on the hunt for something.

"Sable, what are you looking for?"

"Pasta. I don't care what kind. Do you have any?"

I reach around her to one of the top cabinets and hand her some rigatoni.

"Perfect, we'll have chicken alfredo." She moves with purpose, chopping, mixing, and cooking in no time. I have a plate of chicken alfredo in front of me with freshly grated parmesan cheese.

"Mmm... This is great," I tell her, then take another bite. I would never have thought with what I had in the fridge you would have been able to come up with a meal like this."

She takes the bar stool beside me with her plate. "What do you eat when you're training?"

"This would be a good meal; I would just add another piece of chicken with it and a vegetable. No deserts." I take another bite. "Why do you ask?"

"I was just thinking maybe once in a while, I could cook your dinner and bring it to you... unless you have someone that cooks for you when you're training."

"No, I usually wind-up cooking for myself, but I like that idea. Then I could see you."

I don't miss the blush on her cheeks and how her eyes divert toward the floor like a submissive. I reach over and cup her cheek. "We won't be apart the entire three months leading up to the fight. I won't be able to stay away that long."

We eat the rest of dinner in silence while holding hands. We clean up the kitchen and load the dishwasher when we are done. "I need to get home. You're getting up early in the morning. I'm going to grab my bag." She walks into the bedroom, and I fight the urge to follow her and not let her leave.

"Let me walk you home," I tell her as we head out the back door, across the backyard and through the gate. We enter the kitchen of her home.

"Thanks for walking me home," she says, setting her bag on the table.

"I'll call you tomorrow and see how your day went," I tell her, pulling her in for a kiss. "If you need something, call me."

She doesn't say anything, just nods. I could see her name on the book she had just finished reading. "What are you going to be doing? I have a follow-up with a couple of fighters I know. We will have to get verification from the attorneys so that we can even question them."

"Good night, Sable." I lean down and kiss her deeply.

"Night, Matt. I'll call you tomorrow."

"Okay."

I leave out Sable's back door, and she locks it behind me. As I shut the gate, I see her standing at the door, still watching me. I wave at her, and she waves back before closing the curtain.

When I get in the house, I call Eddie. "We are going to make some changes to this training schedule."

"What are you talking about?"

"I'm going to still have time to see Sable," I tell him.

"Matt, man, your job before a piece of ass, you know

the rules. Hell, you made the rules to ensure we wouldn't have any problems like this."

"I'm not fucking around Eddie: either I see Sable or I pull myself out of the fight."

"Wait, what?"

"You heard me. Can you go through the tapes and pull me the title fights of Oratorio and any losses he's had."

"Sure, do you want to watch them with your trainer?"

"No, I'm going to watch them with Sable. She has the best eye I have seen for picking up things about the way people fight."

"I hope the hell you know what you are doing, Matt. This is going to be the greatest fight you've ever had." Eddie sounds worried.

"I'll see you in the morning, Eddie." I hang up the phone.

eleven

MATT

WITH MY RUN THIS MORNING, I HAVE BEEN AT IT FOR CLOSE to six hours. My body and mind are tired as Eddie pulls up in front of my house. There is a glorious smell coming from inside my home.

"What is that smell?" Eddie asks me.

"I don't know." I walk inside to find Sable in the kitchen, swaying her hips side to side with the beat of the music. Several aluminum pans sit on the counters, and the stove has different pots on each burner, bubbling away.

"Sable?" She doesn't hear me. I walk over and turn down the music. "Sable, what are you doing?"

"Shit!" She jumps when she hears me. "You scared the piss out of me."

"What are you doing?" I step up, pulling her into my arms.

"I'm meal prepping for you for the week. I wanted to ensure you were eating right while you were in training, so I talked to a dietician friend, and she said the amount of protein, carbohydrates, and vegetables you eat is significant. I know you would rather call and have food delivered than cook, so this way, you only have to heat it." She looks up at me with those big dark eyes.

"How did you get in?" I ask.

"Your backdoor was unlocked." She steps back out of my arms. "I overstepped, didn't I?"

Eddie smarts off, "You think?"

"Shut up, Eddie. I'll see you tomorrow," I snap at him.

"I'm sorry, I'll go." Sable pulls away from me, the hurt clearly on her face.

"Hold on. I want to talk to you." I turn to see Eddie still standing there. "Good night, Eddie." I point at him.

"Fine." He turns and leaves the room. We hear the front door close as he goes outside.

"Listen, I'm sorry. I'll clean up the mess and get out of here. I thought I would be done by the time you were home. It won't happen again."

She opens her mouth to continue talking; I kiss her to keep her quiet. "Are you going to be quiet and listen now?"

She nods.

"I'm not mad that you are here. I appreciate you

doing all this cooking for me even though you didn't need to." I draw her closer to me, raising her chin so she looks at me. "More importantly, I was thrilled to open my door and see you here waiting on me to come home."

"Can I talk now?" she asks.

"Yes."

"I just wanted to help you and ensure you were taken care of. I meant what I said about not interrupting your training schedule. I just thought this would be a way I could help you." She takes a step out of my arms. "Let me finish this up and clean up the mess, and I'll get out of here."

"Won't you stay a while?"

"Matt, you know why I won't." Once she finishes cleaning, she says, "Your dinner is in the oven heating up. It will be done in twenty minutes." She puts her hands on my cheeks, pulling me in for a kiss. "Bye, Matt."

"I don't like you saying goodbye."

"I'll see you later."

"That's no better."

She turns and walks out the back door. I watch as she crosses the yard and goes through the gate, closing it behind her. I walk out the back door, open the gate, and into Sable's backyard. I knock on her back door. She doesn't answer. I open the door.

"Sable, I'm coming in." I walk into her home, looking around for her. "Sable, where are you?" The thought of hurting her feelings after everything she has done for me kills me. Taking out my phone, I dial Sable's number. Her phone rings upstairs. She doesn't pick up. I head upstairs, calling out her name as I go.

Her phone goes to voicemail. I begin to worry as to why she isn't picking up. I hear water running and realize she is in the shower. Not wanting to scare her to death, at finding me in her home when she gets out, I hurry back downstairs and outside. I take a seat on her back patio and wait.

A few minutes later, my phone rings. "Hello, I'm sitting on your back porch, hoping you will come out and talk with me."

The back door opens, and Sable walks out with her hair still damp, hanging loose down her back.

"Hi."

"Hi, what are you doing here, Matt?" she asks, taking the seat across from me.

"Like I was trying to tell you, I liked coming home and finding you in my kitchen."

"You did, did you? Eddie didn't seem to like the idea." She sits back in her chair, pulling her legs up under her body and getting comfortable. "I won't interfere with your training, Matt. This fight is so important. I know I shouldn't have been there earlier."

"Can I speak now?" I get out of my chair and go to her, kneeling in front of her. "I don't want to stay away from you. I want to see you. What if we have dinner together every night, or at least as often as possible?"

"Eddie is going to lose his mind." She smiles at me, then leans in and kisses me.

"It's good he works for me and not the other way around."

"I'm serious; if you have fight stuff or I have work stuff, we text and let the other know we can't make it. Careers come first for now. Deal?" She touches my cheek with her palm.

"Deal." I take her hand, kissing her palm. "Dinner starts tonight, though, right?"

"Well, I did cook all day." She smiles at me, taking my hand, and I stand with her.

"Do you need anything in the house before we return to my place?"

"No, we need to get dinner out of the oven before it burns."

We walk back through the gate. I don't even bother to close it. Walking into the house, it smells like garlic and chicken— the best Italian restaurant imaginable. "What did you cook?"

"I made chicken lasagna with vegetables; Can you make a salad while I finish with the garlic bread?"

"I can." I get the lettuce, tomatoes, cucumber,

olives, and parmesan cheese out of the fridge, and put them on the counter. I look over my shoulder and see Sable leaning against the bar, watching me. "What are you smiling at?"

"A man helping out in the kitchen is sexy to me." She takes an olive I offer her, simultaneously taking my fingers in her mouth and sucking on them.

"Hmmm..." escapes me at the indication that desert might come before dinner.

"Nope, back to making the salad," she says, swatting me on the ass with the hand towel she is holding.

"I see how this is going to go." I go back to making the salad. "The truth comes out... you see me as a sexual play toy."

Sable laughs out loud. It's the most beautiful sound. I finish the salad as she plates the lasagna and garlic bread. I pour her a glass of wine while I'm drinking water.

"I could have had water, Matt."

"Nonsense, I'm fine with you drinking wine." I take a bite of the lasagna. "Where did you learn to cook like this?" I quickly grab another bite.

"Classes, I don't like to eat out alone, but I like good food, so I figured, why not learn how to cook what I like to eat?" Her face shows pride when she smiles.

"Baby, we can cook together anytime. I would

rather do that than go out as well." I pull her onto my lap. "Thank you for dinner."

"You're very welcome. Let's clean up so that you can walk me home."

"You don't want to be dessert?" I wiggle my eyebrows at her.

She giggles. "I would love to be desert, but I know you're in training, and part of this means you try to stay celibate. So, no dessert for you."

"I should have never told you that during the inter-view." She gets off my lap. "You are going to have me tied in knots by the time this fight is over."

"I'm going to have you ready to win, so I am your prize."

"What if I lose?"

"Then I'm still going to be here either way."

After we clear the table, I walk her to the gate, not wanting to release her hand. "Good night, Sable."

She leans up on her tiptoes. "Good night, Matt." She walks through the gate across her yard and into her house. She gives me a wave as she locks her back door and pulls the blinds closed.

The following month leading up to this fight is going to kill me. I've never wanted to be with a woman as I do her. Eddie isn't helping. If I even mention Sable to him, he wants to hire some piece of ass for me to fuck, thinking that will scratch some itch I have and get my head back into my training.

The way our schedules have been working, it has been almost two weeks since we have spent more than ten minutes together. Sable is doing great with her new career. We didn't expect her to fly all over the country to do it. Or I didn't expect her to be gone all the time is a better way of putting it. She is so happy when we talk on the phone, and you can tell she loves her job. It's everything she has worked for.

Sable is supposed to be off this weekend, and I've told Eddie I'm taking the weekend off. He started to voice his opinion until I threatened to fire his ass if he didn't understand he works for me, and this is what I'm doing.

Being celibate while training has never been that much of an issue until having Sable in my life. I can't get enough of her. I want... No, I need to be with her.

twelve

SABLE

I can't believe I have been traveling for most of the last month. If I'm not traveling then I'm at Club E. All my hard work has paid off and I have finally achieved the career I have always wanted. I have spoken with Ms. Sally and she understands and supports my decision to leave Club E. I will always stay in touch with her, however, since being with Matt, I can't bring myself to be with another man.

I have been following the training of the newest MMA fighters that are thought to be the future champions. My interviews with Matt and Oratorio opened doors for me.

Visiting the dojo that Matt began to train at when he was six touched me emotionally. I figured I would see a lot of cute little kids fumbling around trying to learn the beginning of self-defense. I couldn't have been more wrong.

The kids were cute, and they did have some fumbles but the dedication, the sheer determination these young people were investing in learning and perfecting each move was amazing to watch.

I started with the five-year-old class and spent one day with each age group. When I reached the sixteen-to-eighteen class, it was clear the young people were professionals. They were well aware of what was going to be required of them to go pro.

It wasn't the parents pushing the kids to succeed and practice. I watched them going to school, going to work, and still making it to their practice no matter what time it was.

Some grown-ass people don't have that kind of drive in their lives. As I was talking to Matt about when our schedules would line up, I would tell him about the kids, he said he had some ideas and would like to talk when we see each other.

I have to admit as I sit here on the plane that I'm excited to see Matt. I wasn't going to allow myself to develop feelings for him. The more I told myself this was nothing serious the more I began to fall.

My time away from him, not being able to see, touch, and taste him has driven me insane. Talking with him on the phone made me crave him more. I have decided that this weekend I'm going to tell him the truth about Club E. I need to know how he is going to react before we go any further.

I decide to close my eyes for the last few minutes of my flight and try to relax, Gabby is going to pick me up at the airport, so I don't have to worry about getting an uber. I need to make sure and find time to check in with Ms. Sally since I'm back. I need to see how things are going.

The flight attendant announces our landing and the weather temperature in L.A. is eighty-two degrees. As we taxi up to our gate, I check to make sure I have my phone and have not left anything in the empty seat next to me.

thirteen

SABLE

OUR DOOR OPENS AS WE COME TO A COMPLETE STOP. I GET A text from Gabby telling me she is here. I only have a carry-on since I will be meeting back up with the crew on Tuesday.

I disembark and head to the front of the airport to meet Gabby. Instead of her, a man in a black suit holds a piece of cardboard with my name on it. Cautiously, I walk up to him. "I'm Sable Wagner."

"Your car is this way. May I carry your luggage?"

"Hmmm... One minute." I hold up one finger to get him to give me a moment to call Gabby. "Where are you?"

"Get in the damn car, Sable! Don't ruin the surprise." Gabby hangs up the phone.

"Lead the way," I say to the driver, wondering what Gabby is up to.

We rush out of the airport just as the backdoor of the limo opens.

Matt leans out, looking lickable. "Hey, lady, wanna go for a ride?"

I can't help but laugh. He looks so damn sexy with his grin, knowing he pulled off a surprise. He slowly climbs out of the car and tugs me into his arms. "Finally." That is all he says before he kisses me.

We get in the car, neither one of us saying anything. He hasn't let go of my hand since I arrived. I look at him worried something is wrong. "Is everything all right?"

Without saying anything, he puts up the center divider between us and the driver. Turning, he pulls me onto his lap. "I need to be inside you. I've missed you."

"I've missed you as well." I place my palm against his cheek. "What about your training, your celibacy?"

"I'm taking the weekend off," he announces before assaulting my mouth again, nipping at my bottom lip. "Do you have anything you have to do this weekend, or do we have the entire three days together?"

"I'm yours until seven am Monday morning." I kiss him gently. "Matt, there is something I want to show you when we get to my house."

"Do you want to start showing me here and finish when we get there?" He kisses my neck.

"Ha ha..." I gently push him back. "I'm being serious."

We arrive at my house and go inside.

"You wait down here. I'll be down in a few minutes to show you something." I kiss him deeply. As I begin to walk up the stairs, I stop and look back over my shoulder at him. "Don't go anywhere."

I open my closet, retrieving the outfit I wore at Club E the night Matt was there. I use my orange blossom body lotion then I zip up my boots and get to work on braiding my hair, which only takes a few moments, then I wind it into a bun on top of my head.

I line my eyes with my blackest liner and thicken my lashes after giving my eyes a smokey effect. I top my look with ruby red lipstick and a clear gloss to cause them to shimmer in the light. I stand looking at myself in the mirror. My hands tremble... *Matt may not like this part of me. This might cause me to lose him.* I lightly touch my mask, the last piece of the puzzle of Madame E.

While putting on the mask, the excitement of what is about to take place fills my body with need. Picking up my riding crop, I open the door and walk to the top of the stairs, stopping abruptly.

Matt looks at his phone. I hear an angry, "What the fuck?" As I slowly begin to descend, he turns and sees me, the look on his face isn't what I expect.

"Damn, Sab..." His eyes meet mine. "I wanted it to

be you. You were at the club." His tone isn't surprised. *He might have already known.*

"Did you send me this?" He turns his phone to me, showing a photo of me as Madame E. Underneath it says 'I wonder what the TV station will think of their new sports reporter now?'"

"Oh, my gawd?" I can't stop the tears as they begin to fall. "Who sent you that? I'm ruined."

"We will figure it out." He takes me in his arms and wipes at my tears.

"I wanted to tell you about this, but I was afraid."

Matt sniffs the air. "Orange Blossoms."

I don't say anything just nod my head.

"Why would you be afraid to talk to me?" Matt asks, rubbing his hands down my arms to comfort me. "I should have asked you."

"Why?"

"I suspected but wasn't a hundred percent sure. I had hoped it was you."

"You, hoped?" I look at him.

"I was as attracted to Madame E as I am to you." He places my hand on his jeans, where I can feel his rock-hard cock.

"I wasn't sure how you would react if I told you. You said you were dominant when we first met, but you haven't been that way since we've been together."

"We don't have deep conversations about anything but our careers, do we?"

"I would like that to change this weekend. I want you to know it all. I am or I was Madame E... I'm a switch."

"I recall you saying that and a lot of other things."

"I love to dominate but I also love to submit. I would like to begin playing more deeply with you on a more emotional level. I'm falling in love with you, Matt."

I sit down on the couch and watch him. He's not talking or looking at me. I can feel the tears threatening again. I risk my heart by pushing too hard. I should have taken it slower. "Matt..."

He holds his hand up to me as if to ask me to be quiet. Slowly making his way to me, he takes my hand in his and pulls me up to face him. "What did you say?"

"I love to dominate?"

"No, the last part about your feelings for me." He holds both of my hands in his.

"I'm falling in love with you." A tear slides down my cheek as I confess my feelings for him.

"I've never had someone say that to me that I believe." He takes his thumb and wipes away my tear. "People are always spewing words. Whatever they think you want to hear to get close to you, hoping it will somehow benefit them, but not you. I feel it right here."

He places our hands over his heart. "I feel the same way; I just didn't know how to tell you."

He drops to his knees in front of me. "I have wanted to give you control since the day I saw you at the club. There is something about you in this outfit. The thought of pleasing you completely consumes me." He takes the submissive possession on the floor. His head is down, on his knees, his palms ups.

I'm humbled and honored that a man as strong as Matt would give me the control over him. I take the riding crop and tap him under his chin to get him to look at me. "Matt, do you have safe words?"

"I've always had my submissive use yellow and red."

"We can use yellow and red." I walk around his body, dragging the crop along his shoulders and neck. "Take your shirt off." Matt quickly does as he is told and takes his position again.

I take my mask off. Standing in front of him, I place my foot on his crotch and gently apply pressure with my boot. "I want you to stand and strip." I remove my foot and take a step back.

He stands, stripping off his jeans and boxers. "Let's go upstairs."

He walks in front of me, and I smack him with the riding crop, leaving a red welt across his buttocks.

He wiggles as he struts up the stairs. When we enter the bedroom, I go to my dresser and get my leather straps and cuffs. "Lie on your back in the middle of the bed.

Matt lies back. I take his left wrist and put the handcuff on him and connect it to the gold ring on the headboard, then go to the foot of the bed and do the same thing to his ankle with the leather strap hooked to the ring on the footboard. I move to the other side and do his wrist and ankle.

I run the crop down his naked body and watch him grow harder. "How are you doing, baby?" I crawl up his body to straddle his cock, rubbing against him. I can't help but giggle when his eyes pop wide open at the realization that my body suit is crotchless. "Do you like my surprise?"

"Oh, yeah."

Leaning down, I kiss him hard. I scoot up and straddle his face, hovering just out of his reach. Every once in a while, I allow him a quick taste but nothing more. I turn around and grab his cock in my hands.

Then take Matt into my mouth and down my throat as far as I can. He groans and I stop what I'm doing. Climbing off the bed, I go into the bathroom without saying a word to Matt.

I change my clothes, putting on some shorts and a T-shirt. Walking back into the bedroom, I loosen the straps and clamps holding Matt in place and ask, "I'm hungry, are you?"

I turn to walk out of the room and downstairs. I sit on the couch with my phone, pulling up the menu for a Mexican restaurant that delivers.

Matt stomps down the stairs. "What the fuck, Sable?"

"What?"

"What the hell? You leave me with a fucking hard-on?" he shouts.

"I control when you got to finish." I continue scanning the menu.

"You stopped."

"I know. I'm hungry. Does Mexican food sound good to you?"

Pulling his shirt on, he flops down on the couch next to me. His frustration radiates off of him.

I crawl onto his lap. "Matt, controlling your excitement and your release is part of your submission. It's not meant to torture you." I kiss him. "Well, not torture you too much."

I climb off his lap and sit next to him. "Now what do you want for dinner?"

"Just order a mixture of everything," he says, standing. "I'm going to grab a beer. Do you want one?"

"Yes, please." I order a ton of food and pull my legs

up under me and get comfortable. When Matt sits down, I ask him, "How has training been going?"

"It's going well. I'm feeling good about where I am at this time." He takes my hand into his. "I've missed you."

"I've missed you."

"I was wanting to talk to you about an idea I had. Is it a good time?"

"Of course."

"You have been doing some amazing work recording the kids and it's gotten me thinking of starting a dojo here in L.A. I know it would take a lot of work, but it would be a way to give back to the community and to help up-and-comers to get the training they need."

I don't say anything for a moment, just look at him. "You don't like the idea?"

"I think it's a fantastic idea. You will be an amazing success." There's a knock at the door. "That must be dinner," I tell him as I get up to go answer the door.

Matt goes to the kitchen and gets some plates and a couple more beers. We sit on the floor while we eat and talk about Matt's idea for his new business adventure.

We eat and talk; it's comfortable— by far the best evening I have had in a long time. I'm wanting to move the evening back to the bedroom, but I don't think Matt is ready for that yet. I lean into Matt's chest. "Are you still angry with me?"

"I'm not angry, I just have blue balls."

"No, you don't. You're just used to being in charge. It's very freeing to let someone else be in charge if you just let go and let it happen."

"I don't know if I'm able to do that." He looks upset.

"The real question is are you willing to give it a try? That's the first step." Standing, I hold my hand out to him. "Make love to me, Matt."

The next few hours are spent with us pleasuring each other. No one dominating the other. No submission needed to feel pleasure. Just doing whatever feels right.

fourteen

SABLE

I wake to find the other side of the bed empty. I touch the sheets, and they're cool to the touch, indicating Matt has been up for a while. I go to the restroom and put on my robe before going downstairs in search of the man I'm in love with.

Walking toward the kitchen, I stop when I hear Matt on the phone.

"Eddie, I'm telling you I'm going to do this fight and take some time off to spend with Sable. I want a future with her."

My heart swells at hearing him say how he feels. That's what I want too. *Why is Eddie so against the two of us being together?*

I stop to hear what else Matt is going to say. "Eddie, what the hell is your problem? You have been with me through it all. You know how much all this means to me. There is no way I will let anything get in my way of winning."

My phone vibrates in the pocket of my robe. I have a text from a number I don't know. I open it and it's photos of Matt with several different women. He is in different sex scenes with them. Sometimes multiple partners at a time. The photos are date stamped within the last month. The last photo is dated the night before I came home.

I don't even realize tears are falling down my cheeks until Matt walks in and wants to know what is going on. "I've never asked you to not see other people, Matt, but... you just told me you were beginning to have feelings for me and yet you were fucking someone else twenty-four hours ago?"

"What the fuck are you talking about?" Matt crosses the room to me. "You are the only person I have had sex with since the night at Club E."

"Then explain these." I hand him my phone.

"Those are old photos." He runs his hands through his hair frustratedly. "Who the fuck sent those to you?"

"If they're old, why is the last one dated the day before yesterday?" I'm trying to remain calm, but I'm not doing a very good job of it. My handshakes as I jerk my phone out of his hand.

"Sable, you need to trust me here. I don't know what's going on. I haven't been with anyone."

"I think it's better if I go back on the road and get back to work. That will give you time to figure things out. Eddie doesn't want us together, Matt. Maybe you and I both need to take some time and think about what we each want. Someone is definitely against us being together, they sent you the photo of me as Madame E and now these." I hold my phone out toward him.

"I want you." He steps toward me.

"Stop! Don't Matt, I can't. I never let anyone in. I let you in and this is what happens." I walk to the kitchen opening the back door. "Just go, please go."

Without saying a word, he walks out the kitchen door and across the yard. He makes a call as he walks through the gate into his yard. I sit down on the kitchen floor and cry.

This is why I never let anyone get close. Letting them in gives them the opportunity to hurt me. I should have stayed behind the mask. That way, I don't have to deal with emotions. There, my heart is protected. I'm safe.

My phone rings. I don't even look to see who is calling, I just set it on the table and head upstairs. I'm taking a shower when I hear my name being called. "Sable, Sable? Damn it, girl, you better answer me. Where the fuck are you?"

I wrap a towel around my body and open the bathroom door to find Gabby standing there. "Why the fuck didn't you pick up when I was calling you?"

"I was in the shower."

"Don't give me that shit. I've been calling you for an hour. What the hell is going on? Matt called me and told me to get over here and stop you from leaving town until he can figure out what is going on."

"He shouldn't have brought you into it." I sit on the edge of the bed.

She sits beside me and puts her arm around my shoulder. "He shouldn't have called me." I look at her; I can't hold the tears back anymore.

"You should have called me, Sable. You should always be the one that calls me." Gabby pulls me into a hug. "Get dressed, I want to see these pictures and that text. I need to know whose balls I'm going to cut off: Matt's or someone else's." She takes her fingers and makes a motion as if she is cutting something.

I don't know how she has done it, but she gets me to laugh. "Phones on the table. I'll be down in a minute."

Gabby leaves the room and goes in search of my phone and the victim of her revenge.

I dress and come down to find Gabby on her laptop. "What are you doing?"

"I'm clearing Matt's name."

"What..." I plop down in a chair next to her.

"Sable look at this picture dated two days ago." She turns the laptop toward me.

"No, thank you. I don't need to see Matt with two women." I start to get up and she reaches out and grabs my arm.

"Sable, he's telling you the truth. Someone is jerking you both around." She pulls on my arm until I sit back down. "I want you to look at this picture from over a year ago." I look closely at the photo where Gabby is pointing. It's the same women, the same room, the same everything.

The one different thing is the photo I'm looking at is on Matt's Instagram account from fourteen months ago with a heading of a weekend in Vegas with the guys. I grab my phone and look at the pictures compared to the photos on the Instagram account. They are all on there on different dates than the ones I received.

I send a text to Matt.

ME:

Can you come over so we can talk?

I get up and go to the kitchen, looking out the window while I'm waiting on him to respond. I hear the gate open and see him walking through it.

He sees me and asks, "Can I come in?"

"Yes," I tell him. I hate that there is this strange awkwardness between the two of us.

My phone dings, indicating I have an instant message.

ORATORIO:

Hi, Sable. How are you doing? I was wondering if you would like to go to dinner and catch up?

I can't believe what I'm reading. I release an angry huff, as I realize who's involved in sending me the photos of Matt. I don't believe in coincidences.

"What's wrong who is it?" Matt asks, following me into the dining room.

"Gabby, I think I have the balls you were so eager to cut off earlier." I hand my phone to her, and she reads the text message.

"Oh, he's going to fucking pay. Give me a second, let me check something." Gabby goes to click on the keys of the laptop furiously.

"Can someone explain what is going on?" Matt takes the seat next to Gabby at the table.

"The text I just got was from Oratorio asking me to go out to dinner with him."

"He knows we're together. Everyone knows we are together," Matt says angrily.

Gabby and I both see when Matt realizes what we are talking about. "Son of a bitch! I'm going to kick his ass."

"Wait, I have a better idea," I tell him. "What if we let him think we have split up and that he has won? Then the day of the weigh-ins, I show up with you so we can get into his head before the fight."

"I'm going to fuck with him online," Gabby announces.

"Are you sure it's him?" Matt asks. Gabby turns the laptop toward Matt and me one more time. "This is Oratorio's text history on his phone."

"How the hell do you know how to do that?" Matt asks. "Never mind, I don't want to know, so I can deny any knowledge."

"Gabby is a hacking genius. You just can't tell anyone." I brag about my friend.

Gabby looks at Matt and grins.

"Can you find out who sent me the photo of Sable as Madame E.?" Matt asks Gabby, handing her his phone.

Gabby takes Matt's phone and does something on her laptop. She suddenly stops. "I'm going to go home so I can finish having some fun and set up some interesting things to happen for the next couple of weeks." She pulls me into a hug. "Talk to him," she whispers into my ear.

"I will." I hug her. "Let me know when you are set up so I can respond."

"You got it, girl." She walks up to Matt. "It's a good

thing she loves you and I like you." He pulls her into a hug. "Thanks for calling me and looking out for her."

Matt hugs her tighter. "Thank you."

I follow Gabby as she walks to the door. "Walk me to the car?" Gabby suggests.

"Matt, I'll be right back." He nods his head in agreement. "We reach Gabby's car, are you going to tell me what you found out?"

"The photo was sent to Matt by Eddie." Gabby takes my hand in hers. "Now don't get mad at me... Eddie and I had bumped into each other at lunch one day. I wanted to keep an eye on Matt because he was known to be such a player."

"Gabby what did you do?"

"Eddie went to talk to someone and left his phone on the table. I downloaded my cloning app to it so I could keep an eye on Matt through Eddie."

"Gabby, I should be pissed at you, but what did you find out?"

"Eddie is the one that sent the picture to Matt of you as Madame E." She reaches out, putting her hand on my arm. Gabby leans against her car. "How would Eddie know about Madame E?"

"He comes to the club, but he and I have never run into each other there."

Matt comes out on the porch. "Is everything all right?"

"You want me to come back in as you tell him?" Gabby asks.

"No, this is something I need to do." I turn, looking back at Matt, my heart breaking for him.

Gabby stands, pulling me into a hug. "Call me if you guys need anything. I love you, girl."

"Thanks for always having my back, Gabby. I love you."

Matt takes my hand when I walk up and we go inside. I lead us to the couch to have a seat.

"I'm sorry I didn't listen to you, and I jumped to conclusions about the photos. I hope you and I can work through this."

Matt looks up at me, his eyes filled with hurt. "We have done things all wrong together, haven't we?"

"What do you mean?" I'm afraid he is going to call any chance of us off.

"We didn't date. We jumped right into bed and right to caring for each other." He turns his body so he's facing me. "Sable, I don't want to lose you, but we can't keep going the way we are. We're never going to make it long-term if we don't change a few things. We are giving people too many opportunities to pull this kind of crap with us."

"Gabby knows who sent you the photo of me," I tell him as I take his hand in mine.

"Who?"

"She actually cloned his phone at lunch one day when they ran into each other. She wanted to keep an eye on you so she could look out for me. She's always been there for me and had my back."

"Sable, who sent it?" His grip on my hand tightens.

"Eddie."

"I'm going to kill him. He is the one that gave me the card to come to the fucking club." He jumps up from the couch, instantly letting go of my hand. Matt suddenly turns to me. "Has Eddie ever been one of your clients?"

"I am sworn to secrecy as to who our clients are, but I can tell you who isn't, and Eddie has never been a client of mine."

"Thank gawd." He tugs me to stand and into his arms. "I will get to the bottom of why."

"I know you will."

"Gabby and you can handle Oratorio until the fight. I will handle shit in the ring." He squeezes me tighter. "The thought of you going on a date with him is killing me."

"I'm not going to date him." The thought of being next to him in a car causes my skin to crawl after what he pulled at the club. He seemed like a decent enough guy, but he clearly showed he is a creep. "I'm going to lead him on through text and e-mail."

"Thank the fuck." He kisses my forehead.

"After you win the championship, do you want to go on a date?" I ask him.

He gives me that sexy grin of his. "What do you have in mind?"

"I've never been on a normal date," I confess to him.

He looks at me curiously. "What kind of normal date are you talking about?"

"I want to go bowling, have a beer, and whatever junk food they serve there," I respond excitedly.

"Bowling... I have bowled once. That sounds like fun. Do you have paper and a pen?" he asks.

"Sure." I go to the counter and get the items. "Here you go."

He begins to write:

1. Bowling
2. Movies
3. Ice Skating
4. Fishing

"How do these four things sound to begin with?"

I grab paper and scissors, then cut his list into pieces. "What are you doing?"

I put the cut paper into a vase on the table. "We'll pull something out of the vase and that will be the date we go on, as we think of new things, we add them to the vase."

"I really like this idea," I tell him. "Matt, I'm so sorry."

"There are only two people to blame for this, and we are going to make them pay." He pulls me toward him and onto his lap as he sits on the couch.

My phone dings, telling me I have another message. I pick it up off the coffee table, turning it over to show Matt that it's Oratorio. I lean back against Matt, opening the text to see what it says.

ORATORIO:

> Hi. Thought I would check in and see if you and I can get together and maybe go to dinner and hang out.

"I can't believe the fucking nerve of this dirtbag." I toss my phone down on the couch.

Matt reaches across me and picks up my phone. "We have to respond. You need to get him interested. That's part of the plan, remember?"

I take the phone from him. "I don't know what to say."

"Let's come up with it together. What would you say to avoid him but not offend him?"

> **ME:**
> I'm at the airport, headed back to Washington for work.

> **ORATORIO:**
> I thought you were in town for the entire weekend.

> **ME:**
> I was but... Things changed with Matt and me...

I stop texting and look at Matt, tears in my eyes. "I can't do this."

"Yes, you can. Look at what he sent you. He tried to break us up. Do I need to call Gabby?"

That last statement causes me to laugh. "Are you seriously threatening to call my best friend on me?"

"Yes, I am. I have her number and I'm not afraid to use it." He pulls his phone out of his pocket.

"Okay, I'm texting." I lean over, giving him a quick kiss. "Thank you."

> **ME:**
> Matt and I broke up. I had to get out of town.

> **ORATORIO:**
> I'm so sorry. Do you want to talk about it?

ME:

No. I just want to forget it all.

ORATORIO:

I'm here if you need anything. I can be
on a plane at a moment's notice if you
need me to be.

He puts a heart emoji at the end of his text.

ME:

Thank you.

My phone rings and it's Gabby. "Put me on speaker-
phone. Eddie just got a text that said: 'She's on a plane.
They broke up. I'll meet you with the final payment.'"

"Eddie is working with Oratorio?" Matt growls.

"I don't think going after them both right now is
the smart thing to do," Gabby responds. "Sable, keep
Oratorio talking. Reach out to him and string him
along... I know this isn't something you would ever do
but look at how low he went. If I couldn't do what I can
do with a computer, you would never have known
those photos weren't real. Hun, he would have played
you." Gabby takes a deep breath that we can hear on
the phone. "Matt, you can't risk going after Eddie right
now. We need to know more."

"Thanks for always keeping me straight," I tell
Gabby.

"I've always got your back. Love you. Night, Hey Matt..."

"Yes."

"I'm sorry."

"Night, Gabby. Thank you," we both say to her before I hang up.

Matt stands up and walks to the door. He shuts off the porch light and the front room light. "What are you doing?"

"I'm making it look like you aren't home." He shuts off the lamp on the table. "We can go to my house. Everyone expects me to be home."

"Thank goodness you and Gabby are thinking tonight. I'll go up and grab a few things to bring over." I turn on the flashlight on my phone.

I'm upstairs putting some clothes in a duffle bag and some items out of the bathroom when I get a text on my phone.

MATT:

Stay upstairs and shut your light off. Someone just pulled into the driveway.

I quickly shut off my light and go to the top of the stairs. A flashlight shines in my windows downstairs. I'm shaking, wondering where Matt is. I hear someone coming up the stairs toward me. "Sable?"

"I'm right here, at the top."

"Do you have everything you need?" He takes my bag out of my hand.

"Are they still here?"

"Yes, but we are still going out the back way. We'll set your alarm and keep an eye on your cameras, but I want to get you to my house now." He takes my hand and leads me down the dark stairs and out the back door. We stop outside and listen. We hear a car door and then the car starts up. Headlights flood the backyard as the car backs out of the driveway. We wait until the car is gone and go through the gate into Matt's backyard.

"Let's pull up your cameras, I want to know who was at your house."

I fire up my laptop and pull up my cameras. I don't believe my eyes when I see the car pull into the driveway. It's Eddie. Matt's manager and friend. I don't say anything. I just send the photo of Eddie to Gabby to give her a heads-up, before closing the laptop.

I don't even know what to say to Matt. Anger radiates off him. I don't move, I just sit there, not knowing what to say to comfort him and not cause him more pain.

He takes a few deep breaths and walks to me. He pulls a chair out and sits in it, facing me. I turn in my chair to look at him. I place my palm on his cheek.

Kissing my palm, he leans forward and pulls me to him. "I don't understand why he would do this?" he tells me.

"I think Eddie might just want to make sure you are concentrating on the fight; he knows you have wanted this your entire career."

"Sable, I love how sweet you are, trying to take up for Eddie, but he's going to pay. He's going to pay just like Oratorio is going to pay. They messed with the one person that means the world to me." He kisses me gently.

He stands, let's go get some sleep. We head up to Matt's bedroom. "Do you want to take a shower?" he asks.

"I would love to take a shower; it would help us relax."

We walk into the bathroom and begin to help each other undress. Matt turns on the water, adjusting the temperature. He steps in, taking my hand to help me in. The rain shower head above kicks on and the warm water cascades down onto us.

"Let me wash your hair," Matt tells me.

I turn around and lean my head back as he puts shampoo in my hair and lathers it up. Having someone else wash my hair is very relaxing.

To make it easier on me, he sits in the chair at the end of the shower so I can return the favor. We begin washing each other's bodies and things begin to heat up between us.

We finish in the shower and step out. Instead of wrapping up in towels, we repeat the same process as we had in the shower, each drying the other. There is something so sensual about it. I grab the comb for my hair and Matt holds his hand out. "May I, do it?"

"Sure." I hand him the comb. "Matt, do you think we are doing the right thing by leading Oratorio on and not letting Eddie know we are on to him?"

He sits down on the edge of the bed next to me. "Yes, I do. They set out to split us up. I know what Oratorio's motives are. He wants you. Eddie, I can't figure out exactly what he is up to."

"I think Eddie thinks I'm a distraction. The more titles you win, the more money he makes."

Matt puts my comb back in the bathroom. He comes out carrying a T-shirt for me to put on. "Do you want this now or for later?"

"I'll put it on later if I get cold." I climb up the bed, sliding under the sheet. Matt folds down the comforter to the end of the bed before slipping in next to me. We both moan in comfort as to how good the bed feels.

I curl into Matt's side as he wraps his arms around me. "I was so scared I lost you," he whispers with his lips against my ear.

I cling to him tighter. "My heart broke when I saw

those photos. I should have trusted you instead of jumping to conclusions."

"I would have done the same thing." He squeezes me tight. "Thank gawd for Gabby. How did she learn to do all that?"

"When Gabby was a teenager and first got her hands on a computer in class, she just seemed to find her calling. She was always getting in trouble for hacking into the system and changing grades. For a while, she wanted to do computer crimes but then her Instagram and blog took off. By doing social stuff, it keeps her off the cop's radar for hacking."

"Wow, I had no idea she's a computer genius." Matt sounds genuinely impressed.

"She is a marketing genius as well. She is the one that got me the scope on your title fight. Actually, it was Eddie who told Gabby the day you signed the contract for the title fight." I put my hand over my mouth trying to hide a yawn. "Gabby put me in touch with Oratorio's publicist."

"We can talk more tomorrow." Matt leans down to kiss me. We snuggle down for a good night's sleep.

fifteen
MATT

I wake to my phone ringing. I slip my arm from under Sable's neck, so I don't wake her. "Hello," I answer, walking into the hall.

"What are you doing today? Will I see you at the gym?" Eddie asks.

Just as I start to respond, a pair of arms wrap around my waist, hugging me tightly. I look at Sable and she smiles at me, then mouths the words: *stay calm, you got this.*

"Sable kicked my ass to the curb yesterday. Someone sent her photos of me fucking some bitches, and she lost her shit. She jumped on a plane and left town last night"

"Man, that's fucked up. Who do you think did it?" Eddie asks.

"No clue. She took off and went back to Washington right after throwing me out of her house."

"No shit. You need to get out of the house. Why don't we go out and hit the club tonight?"

"No, man, I'm going to take it easy this weekend. I'm going to go for a run, chill, and watch some TV."

"Want me to call some ladies and have them swing by to cheer you up?"

"I've already taken care of it. Have a good weekend. I'll talk to you Monday."

"Sure, man. Later." Eddie hangs up the phone.

I go downstairs to find Sable sitting on the kitchen counter drinking coffee. She picks up a cup and hands it to me.

I take a drink, setting the cup down. I slide between her thighs, pulling her to the edge of the counter. "Good morning." She kisses me.

"Hi, I didn't mean to wake you."

"You didn't, the empty bed did."

"Feeling lonely, were you?" I kiss her neck.

"I was terribly lonely." She kisses my neck and chest.

"We can't have you being lonely now, can we?" Sable shakes her head.

I reach back and pull a chair up so I can sit down. Doing so, I'm now head high with her crotch. I slide my fingers under her T-shirt, slipping them into the elastic of her panties.

Sable raises her hips up so I can slide the panties down her legs and onto the floor.

"Oh, breakfast is served." I look at her legs spread open. I dive in without hesitation. My tongue separates her folds to find the taut nub standing at attention, begging for me to suck on it.

Sable grabs my head and holds it in place when she squirms.

"Yes, yes, right there. Don't stop, gawd don't stop," she keeps repeating as she comes apart. Her legs squeeze on my head, trying to get me to stop.

I pick her up, sit her on the table, then push her back so she lies down. I place her heels up on my shoulders. I don't give her any time to think before I pound into her over and over.

She yells, "I can't hold out anymore. I have to come."

I send her over the edge when I hammer into her harder and harder.

"Yesssss...." That is all I hear her scream out as we both release together.

I help her sit up off the table. "Good morning," I say with a laugh.

"It is now," she says back to me as she slides off the

table to get her coffee. "Matt, I'm worried Eddie's going to show up here."

"So am I."

"I hate to say this, but I might need to get back to Washington so we don't get caught." Sable takes a drink of her coffee and leans against the counter.

"I don't like it." I lean forward, putting my forearms on my knees. "We have a week till the fight. I don't want you to go."

"I don't want to, but we have to stick to the plan. You and Gabby convinced me of this. I want to see what the future will be like with you and me together, but we have to take out the trash before we can move forward."

"I know. How are you with phone sex?" I look at her and grin.

"I guess you're going to find out, big fella."

"Do you need to get stuff from your house before you take off?"

"Just a few things. I can call Gabby and have her pick me up and take me to the airport," Sable states.

"I think it would be better if you have a car pick you up. This way no one sees you being dropped off."

"I can fly out of LAX instead of Burbank. I have less chance of being spotted. Let's face it, there are thousands of people at LAX and a few hundred at Burbank. It's easier to get lost in a crowd."

"You can wear your hair up and a hat as well," I suggest.

"I need to get online and check flights."

"Your laptop is in the other room," I tell her. "I'm going to go upstairs and get dressed." I leave Sable on the laptop, looking into flights.

After a few minutes, I descend the stairs to find the backdoor open and so is the gate to Sable's house. I walk through, taking it slow as I approach her house. The back door isn't closed all the way. I gently slide the door open and look around. I don't find her on the first floor, so I move upstairs. "Sable, are you here?"

"Hey, what are you doing over here?"

"What are you doing here? You're supposed to stay at my house until you leave."

"I had to come get my stuff to take with me." She picks up a carry-on duffle bag and starts for the stairs. She tells me about the flight she found and that she has already contacted an Uber to pick her up in the next thirty minutes.

"Are they picking you up here or at my house?"

"Your house. I told them they had to pull into the garage."

"We need to get back to the house then." I pick up her duffel and check the front door to ensure it's locked before we walk out the back door.

We get all her stuff from my house and sit down

and wait for her driver to show up. Sable's phone lets her know he is approaching the neighborhood. I go out and open the garage. The driver pulls right in. He jumps out when he sees Sable and smiles as he takes her bag from her to put it in the car.

I pull her into an embrace. "Call me when you land."

"I will." She puts her ponytail up in her hat and blows me a kiss before closing her door. I watch the car back out of the garage and as it goes down the road. Emptiness and loneliness fill me and my home now that Sable is gone.

"Fuck!" I say to no one but myself. I go upstairs and change into some sweats for the gym. A workout sounds good as angry as I am.

I'm trying to find someone to spar with but no one wants to get in the ring with me today. They all keep making comments about how I'm too aggressive today for sparring.

I check my phone to see if I have any text messages. I have one from Gabby asking me to give her a call. I dial her number.

"Hey, Matt."

"Hi, what's up? Everything good?"

"Everything is fine. I talked to Sable, and she wanted me to give you a heads up that Oratorio showed up in Washington."

"What the fuck?" I start to lose my temper.

"It's all right, her team took care of her. They told him she was on assignment and would be gone for at least five days and they were getting ready to fly out and meet her. They are going to move on down the coast to Oregon and meet up with an all-female dojo. She'll let me know what hotel she's at as soon as she checks in."

"Thanks for letting me know, Gabby."

"Matt, we have to protect her. Her life has been rough. She deserves to be happy with you."

"We will. Do you want to have some fun?" I ask Gabby as I get an idea.

"What do you have in mind?"

"Lunch, Café Daham, three p.m.?" I suggest.

"Sounds like I have lunch plans. See you soon."

I finish my workout and get ready to go meet Gabby. Café Daham is well known for its privacy and dark corner booths. I walk in, and I'm taken to the back far corner booth the curtains surrounding the booth are pulled closed.

I open them and find Gabby sitting there. "Hi, handsome. I ordered you a juice while I have a cocktail."

"Thanks." The waitress comes and takes our order for lunch.

"What did you have in mind to have some fun?"

I slide a piece of paper across the table to her. Gabby picks it up and looks at it, then at me. "Matt, that's some serious jail time if I get caught."

"I don't want you to actually do it. I want you to make him think it has happened."

"Wait... you want me to make Eddie think his personal bank account has been wiped clean, but you don't want me to really do it? Just make it look like it on paper."

"Can you do it?" I ask knowing it's going to push her buttons.

"Oh, you got jokes. You know damn well I can do this. My girl has told you I have skills, or you wouldn't have thought to come to me with this."

"I want to make sure you are safe, but he needs to suffer. Him thinking he's broke will really fuck with him."

The waitress shows up with our food. We wait until she's gone before we speak again. Gabby keeps messing with her phone and only looks at me when she is done eating.

"What do you think of the idea?"

"I think Eddie is going to worry about scanning his credit card for a while." Gabby laughs.

sixteen

MATT

I wasn't expecting Eddie to be sitting on my porch as I pull up my drive and get out of my car.

"What are you doing here?" I try to sound casual.

"Just thought I would come over and check on you. It doesn't look like you are taking the weekend off and chilling."

"I decided I hit the gym and go for a run. I have a championship to win."

"Damn right you do. I'm glad to see your head is back in the game," Eddie replies.

"What do you mean *back* in the game? I've never lost focus of this fight." My anger grows.

"I just mean that when Sable was around, you didn't seem to concentrate the way you used to," Eddie tries to smooth over his statement.

Taking a deep breath, I answer, "Maybe." I open my door and go inside. Unfortunately, Eddie follows me into the house. "Eddie, what are you doing? I told you I wanted to be left alone for the weekend."

"I..." Eddie is distracted by his phone dinging. "What the hell?" He totally ignores me and concentrates on his phone. "It's all gone," he keeps repeating over and over.

"What are you talking about?" I ask him, to show concern. "Is everything all right, man?" I know damn well Gabby has been having fun by the way he is reacting.

"My money... it's gone." Eddie flops down on my couch.

"How the hell is your money gone?" I take a seat in the chair, trying not to smile at his distress. "Where did it go?"

"I've been hacked." He hands me his phone. "They've taken it all."

"Who would want to hack you? Have you pissed anyone off or do you owe anyone?" I take his phone and read the text message.

ANONYMOUS:

You fucked with the wrong person and now you're going to pay.

Gabby is good at dramatic. "It's just a text... have you checked your accounts?"

"Of course, I checked my fucking accounts. They are empty!" Eddie yells at me.

"Dude, watch it. I didn't take it," I warn him.

"I know, I'm just fucked," he responds, sounding desperate.

"Why are you fucked? Banks are insured. You're being dramatic as always."

"Fuck you, Matt. I owe a lot of money to some people who aren't going to take too kindly to me telling them *'Hey I've been hacked, oops sorry, I don't have your money.'*"

"Eddie, what the fuck are you into?" I ask him.

"It doesn't concern you as long as you win this championship."

"What happens if I lose?" I'm wondering if this is all Gabby's doing or if Eddie is really in over his head.

"Last time we were in Vegas, I may have made a large wager on you taking the title fight against Oratorio and winning it."

"May have made a large wager? Who the fuck are you betting with?"

I take a step toward him, to which he instantly begins to back away. "You know betting on my fights when you are my manager is illegal. You could cost me my title. Do you realize what the fuck you have done?"

I have Eddie's shirt wadded into my fist at his throat. I'm trying to keep myself from beating him to a bloody pulp. "Who do you owe?" I backhand him across his face. "Who the fuck do you owe?"

"Franco... Franco Salvador."

"Oratorio's uncle? He's rumored to have ties with the mob."

"It's not a rumor."

"How much did you bet?" I let go of his shirt.

"Half a million."

"Eddie, you really are a dumb fuck, aren't you?" I walk into the living room and sit down. Putting my face in my hands. "How do you think this is going to affect me and my career?"

"If you don't fight, I'm dead. If you win, I win."

"If I lose? You're dead since you don't have a half million to pay them?" I slam my fist down on the counter.

"Yep." Eddie's shoulders slump and he looks at the floor instead of looking at me.

"You need to get out of here and see if you can figure out who you have pissed off enough that they would go after your money... unless you think Franco is involved to make sure you can't pay." I walk him to the door. "Figure your shit out, Eddie, then you and I are going to talk."

I close the door behind him. I watch him back out of

the driveway. Taking my phone out of my pocket, I call Gabby. "Hey, you work fast."

"I'm that good," Gabby brags.

"We need to meet. Do you want to come here, or do you want me to come to you? We are going to have to call Sable so she can hear as well," I tell her.

"Come here. I'll text you, my address. We can get Sable on Zoom at the same time." She hangs up. My phone dings with the information.

On my way to Gabby's house, I keep thinking about what Eddie told me. If I go to the UFC and tell them everything, the fight will be canceled, but I might be able to keep my titles. I could retire without any bad press.

Am I ready to give up on my dream or risk it with the chance of never having the opportunity to try to get it back?

I pull up to Gabby's and ring the buzzer. She buzzes me in. "Hi, you look like you have the weight of the world on your shoulders. This is supposed to be fun."

"Let's get Sable on so I can tell you both what I just found out." I point to her computer.

Gabby brings her laptop over to the couch and sets it on the coffee table. After a moment, Sable's gorgeous face appears on the screen. "Hi, guys! I miss you both."

"Hi," we both say in unison. "I asked Gabby if we could all talk because Eddie just left my place. I found out a lot of interesting and possibly dangerous things."

I tell both of them everything Eddie and I had discussed. I also tell them I'm thinking about going to the authorities to clear my name before shit hits the fan and that Gabby should clear her hack on Eddie's accounts. Things have gotten really serious in the last couple of hours.

"Matt, I agree with you about Gabby removing her hack, but I'm worried if you go to the UFC and turn this in your career could be over."

"If I don't turn it in and I lose, my career is over, and my name is ruined. I'll never be able to open the dojo we discussed."

"Can I jump in?" Gabby asks.

I turn to face her. "I'll remove the hacks, that's nothing big. I didn't touch his account. I messed with his phone. Eddie's life is on his phone. I won't get into any trouble. You have to go to the authorities; you have too much riding on this. Your future, your reputation— all rides on this, plus they can help to ensure Sable is safe if things with Eddie and Franco go south, they will know she is a weakness of yours and can be used against you."

"I'll be fine," Sable protests.

"You're safe as long as you are out of town and no

one knows where you are, but Gabby's right: I have to come forward. Sable, I'll call you later, so Gabby can get to work removing her hack and cloning program. I want it off before I go to the authorities."

"Okay, talk to you soon." Sable disconnects her video and disappears from the screen of the laptop.

"How long is it going to take you to remove everything?" I lean back, tilting my head back, trying to relax.

"You relax. I'll let you know when I'm done." Gabby picks up her laptop and goes to the dining table.

I close my eyes and think about what I'm going to do. *What am I doing?* I question myself. I know what I'm going to do there has never been any doubt. I love this sport and have dedicated my life to it.

There is no way I can stand back and let people like Eddie and Franco destroy it. I just hope Oratorio isn't in on it. Gabby calls my name, "Matt, I'm all done."

I gave her a quick hug. "You're going to the authorities, aren't you?"

"Yes."

"You're a good man, Matt Jones." Gabby gives me a hug. "You are the right man for Sable, don't you ever doubt it."

"Thanks, Gabby. You're quite the woman."

"Don't I know it? I'm single if you know anyone." She gives me a wink before closing the door.

I drive home without thinking anymore about my decision. I go inside after locking the door and walk straight upstairs to bed. I kick my shoes off and lay down. I'm exhausted, emotionally and physically.

I'm asleep in no time.

seventeen

MATT

THE ATHLETICS COMMISSIONS OFFICE IS LIKE THE PRINCIPAL'S office. Only the bad show up there, or the ones who get praised. At the moment, I'm not really sure what I am, only that it took me two long hours to get to the headquarters in West Los Angeles, and I'm sweating bullets. My entire career rides on what happens here. My friendship... that's a different story. I don't think that's salvageable. Eddie traded my dream for God knows what.

Eddie and I have always had each other's back. No matter what, I have never doubted Eddie's faithfulness. All these years together, Eddie has always been the constant in my career. When I lost my parents, Eddie was there, just as I was for him. We were more than friends, we were brothers.

I walk in and ask to see someone about the upcoming fight.

I'm led into a large conference room with eight men in suits waiting on me. "Mr. Jones, please take a seat. This is highly unusual for a fighter to request to speak to us about their upcoming fight for World Champion," the man at the head of the table says.

"I understand, but these are unusual circumstances I have found myself in. Not knowing exactly where I should turn, I thought going to the top would be the best way to handle it."

"You have our attention, please go on."

For the next four hours, I'm asked questions, asked to leave the room, asked to return to the room so they could ask more questions. I'm finally brought back into the room. "Mr. Jones, we are ready to talk to you again."

I take a seat.

"Mr. Jones, we would first like to thank you for bringing this to our attention as soon as you found out. This speaks a lot about the type of man and character that you possess." Everyone else at the table nods their heads.

"We would like you to continue with the fight."

"Seriously?" I ask confused by what I'm hearing.

"Yes, we are going to continue to investigate what you have brought us, and we will be at the fight with extra security to ensure you and Ms. Wagner are safe.

We do suggest you think about getting a new manager after the fight. We are also requesting you and Ms. Wagner keep this information quiet until we conclude our investigation. If we discover anything that may affect either of you, we will let you know."

I stand to leave, and all the men come around the table to shake my hand.

Walking out of the building, I feel better about my decision. I don't regret coming and talking to the officials. This is the one time I'm going to go into the ring and know it is definitely going to be me putting it all out there. Win or lose, it's time I move on to my future. *Without Eddie.*

I hit the gym as soon as I get back. Eddie joins me midway through my workout. "It's good to see you back with so much determination." Eddie is all smiles.

"Why do you look like you are up to something?"

"I'm just in a great mood," he tells me. "Can't a man be in a good mood?"

"You were freaking out not more than twenty-four hours ago, what changed? Did you win the lottery?" I ask.

"Better, I got all my money back." He struts around as if he has done something heroic.

"How the hell did you pull that off?"

"There was an error with the bank system, my money was never gone." He shrugs his shoulders.

"That's great, Eddie."

"So, you ready to kick Oratorio's ass and take over the World title?"

"There is one thing I have to do before I'm ready to take on the title." I take a step closer to Eddie.

"What's that?"

Without saying anything, I swing left, right, left. Eddie stumbles backward until he hits the wall. Once he is against the wall, my assault on him continues. Three other fighters jump in, one standing between Eddie and me; the other two pushing me back away from him.

"You are fired, mother fucker. If I see you again, I'm going to kick your ass over and over. Stay the fuck away from me."

"What the fuck is wrong with you, Matt? I've always had your back. You think you're going to get anywhere without me helping you?" Eddie spits blood out of his mouth. "Good luck."

"Get him out of here." The other fighters lead Eddie out of the gym. I finish my workout and go home.

eighteen

MATT

IT'S BEEN TEN DAYS, JAM-PACKED WITH TRAINING AND SWEATY gyms, but today I finally get to lay eyes on my girl.

I glance at the watch on my wall eager to feel those lips on mine and wrap my arms around her. She's a couple of minutes late, but I set my watch ten minutes ahead so I'll always be early.

Just as I head toward the kitchen for a bottle of water, there's a knock at the back door. I swing it open to find two goddesses standing there, waving excitedly.

The following week and a half flew by. My life has become very predictable. I wake and train, call Sable and sleep, repeat. Sable comes home tonight, she and Gabby are coming to the weigh-ins.

Oratorio has kept up his chase of Sable. He has been texting and calling her the entire time she has been gone. When she walks in on my arm to the weigh-ins the look on his face is something I can't wait to see.

I'm at home getting ready when I hear the knock at the back door. I walk to the door and open it quickly. "Holy shit, you two are goddesses." I take Gabby's hand and give her a twirl as she enters the house. "I have been missing you something fierce." I pull Sable into my arms.

Gabby instantly stops any moves I have in mind. "Do not mess up her makeup."

"Damn you two are sexy," I tell both women. "You ladies ready to go cause some havoc?"

They both smile and nod their heads. Sable is wearing a very form-fitting black mini dress with Christian Louboutin stilettos. Gabby wears a matching form-fitting red mini dress with Christian Louboutin stilettos.

I am wearing black slacks with a red silk shirt, and black tie, to match both women. We have to be at weigh-ins in forty-five minutes. The limo has arrived to pick us up. We get in and head to the Franklin Center. The ladies enjoy a glass of Champaign as we drive.

The place is packed, and we are taken around back where we can make an entrance at the perfect time. Oratorio is taken out to be weighed first. We manage to stay out of sight until he is on stage. The crowd goes wild, letting me know he has made weight.

It's my turn. Sable and Gabby each take one of my arms as we enter the stage. The crowd goes insane at seeing the three of us together. I begin to unbutton my shirt, never taking my eyes off Oratorio. His mouth hangs open as he sees Sable and Gabby. I watch him as I undress to step on the scale.

Sable looks at him, blowing him a kiss; Gabby follows and does the same thing. Oratorio's face is brought up on the big screen. Everyone can see him standing there staring at Sable and Gabby. I step up on the scale and the crowd goes insane. I had no doubt I'd make the weight.

Oratorio heads straight for Sable, I cut him off and step in front of her. "Save it for the ring," I tell him. Sable bends down picking up my clothes and Gabby has my shoes. I dress standing between Oratorio and Sable. His team pulls him to the other side of the stage.

I take Sable's hand; Gabby wraps her arm through mine, and we leave the center and go out for dinner. After we eat, we drop Gabby off at her place and are taken to mine.

Sable and I walk into the house. I can't resist her any longer. As soon as the door closes, I have her back against the door and claim her mouth. When we break apart, Sable starts to speak.

I put my finger on her lips. "Tonight, I'm in charge. No talking, understand."

Sable nods her head not saying a word.

I know we can't have sex until after the fight but there is nothing in my ritual about Sable orgasming. I carry her upstairs placing her on the bed. I have the bed ready for the night. I have silk rope lying on each corner of the bed.

I slide her down my body till she is standing in front of me. "Strip!" I command her.

"Yes, sir."

Her eyes never leave mine as she removes one piece of clothing at a time. She stands in front of me with only a bra and panties. She slowly pulls down one bra strap and then the other. She reaches around unhooking it, then lets it fall to the floor.

She turns her back to me and slides down her panties with a finger on each side. Bending at her waist as she pulls the panties down her legs and slowly steps out of them. I walk over to her and take them from her.

"I'm going to take these to the fight with me as my good luck piece." She smiles at me approvingly.

"On to the bed, lying on your back." I take her hand, leading her over.

Sable climbs onto the bed, obeying me. She lies down I take her right leg and wrap the silk rope around her ankle and tie it to the loop on the footboard. I do the same to her other leg and both arms.

"Are you comfortable? Lying there looking so delicious."

"Yes, sir."

I strip and put on some basketball shorts. She looks confused. "Tonight, is about you. I want to show you how much I have missed you."

I slowly drag my hand down her body stopping to give each nipple attention. I walk to the end of the bed and take in the vision in front of me. I drop to my knees and crawl up the bed to her. Licking up her legs until I find her center. I waste no time and dive right in. My relentless assault on her clit has Sable crying out as she comes.

"Give me more baby," I tell her and continue not slowing down. Sable's legs shake, and her body twists as she tries to get free of me. "Oh Gawd!" She screams as her juices squirt out of her body covering my face. I continue to lick up her juices but at a gentler pace. Allowing her body to calm.

I get up and go to the bathroom to wash my face and get a warm cloth to clean Sable, ensuring she isn't tender later. I untie her ankles and wrist rubbing each one to make sure there are no marks, and the circulation is restored.

I climb into bed next to her. Her sleepy body rolls into my side and I pull her against me close wrapping her in my arms.

I raise before Sable; I kiss her on the cheek leaving a note for her on the side of the bed. I'm on my way to the gym, I need to get my warmups in before heading to the convention center.

It's strange to be getting ready for the biggest fight of my life and Eddie is not here. I haven't seen him since I fired him. I guess I'm missing the traditions we had before the fight. I'm going through all my warm-up drills when I'm told it's time to head to the stadium.

I'm at the stadium, I ask security to go get Sable and bring her back here. I need to know that she is okay. After ten minutes she is delivered to me by a security guard for the convention center.

"Hi, you." She smiles at me, making me instantly relax. "You got this, Matt. Win or lose, we have each other." She kisses me. "Kick his ass and make him suffer." She turns and walks out the door with the security guard.

A few minutes later, Oratorio's music begins to play and he enters the ring to the cheer of the crowd. I hear my music start. I've always used Highway to Hell by AC/DC for my entrance music on title fights. My energy peaks as I begin my entrance to the ring. I stop and have a quick inspection before climbing between the ropes.

From my corner, I can see Sable sitting directly in front of me. I notice the front row to the right of the ring is all the officials from the UFC commission. I glance to Oratorio's corner and Eddie is sitting there with Franco. Eddie doesn't look very happy.

The official calls us to the center of the ring to give us a rundown of the rules. We are to go back to our corners and come out fighting at the bell.

I remember everything Oratorio has done to try to keep Sable and me apart. How he has called her, trying to manipulate our relationship with those photos. The anger inside me begins to rise. I hear the bell ding and the fight is on.

I leave my corner, heading straight for him. I throw a left, right, and then a kick. I continue my attack never letting him have a moment to regain his composure. I finally have an opening, and I hit him with an uppercut causing his head to jerk backward. Oratorio is on the mat. I'm on top of him not stopping. Punch after punch, I pound on him until his eyes close and the referee jumps in and pulls me off him.

The bell sounds and I'm sent to my corner. Oratorio is still lying on the mat just as the referee begins to count Oratorio gets up. They check him and clear him to continue. I again rush right for him. He swings, and I'm able to dodge it. Oratorio has his back to me for just a moment, which is all I need. I get him in a reverse choke hold. The tighter my hold on his throat gets, the less he fights.

Finally, I feel the tap of his glove on my arm. The

referee tells me to let him go, and Oratorio rolls off of me trying to catch his breath.

The crowd goes insane as my arm is raised in victory. "Ladies and gentlemen, in one minute-thirty-seconds, by submission, Matt Jones is your new World Champion."

Sable is brought into the ring. I wrap my arms around her. "I love you. Will you marry me?" The entire place goes quiet waiting for her to answer.

"Yes," she yells as the crowd erupts again.

I do all the photos I'm required to do along with all my interviews with Sable by my side. When we are in the back, my trainer unwraps my hands as Gabby leads the UFC officials toward us.

"Congratulations, Matt. Hell of a fight. We wanted you to know Oratorio will no longer be able to fight for his involvement in the betting. Your ex-manager, Eddie Langley, is going to jail with his friend, Mr. Franco Salvador. It seems they have been up to quite a bit of illegal activity."

"What about Matt?" Sable asks.

"You did the right thing and came to us right away. You won the fight fairly. You are the new World Champion. Congratulations on the fight and your upcoming wedding." They all turn and leave the room except for Gabby.

"Wedding, shopping, bachelorette party..." She has

her phone out making notes. "We have so much to do. Come on you two let's go celebrate."

"Gabby, go have fun. We are going to celebrate in private. Love you!" Sable pushes her out the door. "Let's go home, Mr. Champion."

198

epilogue

SABLE

It's been six months since Matt won the World Championship and proposed to me. Today is the day we say I do.

We had decided on an intimate ceremony in Hawaii with the people that mean the most to us. Ms. Sally took control of everything; she was not going to be deterred.

The travel arrangements, our suites, even my dress and Gabby's, were designed by her friend and designer Alyson Garbo, who flew to Hawaii to personally deliver our gowns and ensure the fit is perfect.

When Alyson walks into the room, I can't believe my eyes. She used to be one of Ms. Sally's girls when I first went to work at Club E. I knew her as Ali.

Ali's face broke into a huge smile. "I knew you were going to grow up to be a knockout." She pulls me into a hug. "You reached your goal; Sally and I always knew there would be no stopping you."

"You must be Gabby." She gives her a hug as well. "You are going to look gorgeous in what I've made for you." She opens a garment bag to reveal an off-the-shoulder burgundy linen dress with a slit-up Gabby's left thigh.

Ms. Sally enters the room as Gabby makes her entrance in her gown. "Oh Gabby, if you ever want a side gig, you'd make a killing working for me."

"I'll keep that in mind." Gabby smiles, her cheeks turning bright red.

There's a knock at the door. When Gabby opens it, Dante is there looking extremely handsome in his linen pants and a button-down shirt.

"Gabby, you're a vision." Dante kisses her on the cheek. "I have a gift for Sable from Matt." He holds out a small black box.

"Thank you, Dante. Can you take this to Matt for me?" I hand him a small jewelry box. Inside is a gold key on a key ring that says I love you.

I open the box from Matt after Dante leaves the room. Inside is a gold key on a key ring. I start laughing. "What is it Gabby asks?" I hold the key up for everyone to see.

Ms. Sally begins to laugh with me. "You two really are perfect for each other, aren't you?"

A moment later, my phone dings with a message.

MATT:

> I'm guessing we both met with the architect and had the same thing in mind since these are the exact same keys. I love you, Sable. I will see you in a few minutes.

"What do the keys mean?" Gabby asks.

"It means that the man I'm marrying is perfect for me." I hook my key on the garter on my thigh.

Ali walks up with my gown: a trumpet-style bridal gown, featuring a high halter neckline and cutout back and edged with chandelier beadwork on the shoulders. Embroidered lace and scattered beards richly embellish this form-fitting tulle wedding dress, finished with a godet skirt that spills to a semi-chapel train.

I slip into my gown. It fits perfectly. Ali couldn't have gotten the fit any better.

Ms. Sally and Ali take their seats. Gabby starts down the aisle to the wedding march. I follow behind; my nerves disappear as soon as I lock eyes with Matt.

I am confident in my decision of becoming Matt's wife and starting our journey together. I take my time as I slink down the aisle. Linen pants may not have been the best idea for Matt to wear as he sees me in my dress. Thank goodness his shirt is untucked. It slightly covers his cock as it hardens with each step I take.

When I reach the altar, he takes my hands in his. "You are gorgeous. I loved my gift." He puts his hand over his heart and breast pocket.

I touch the blue garter that is visible through my sheer gown drawing Matt's attention to the key hanging from it on my thigh.

The woman marrying us keeps it short and intimate as we had wished. After the ceremony, everyone joins us for a Hawaiian luau. It's wonderful to see our friends laughing and having fun. They will all be leaving the island the next day and heading home.

Matt and I say our goodbyes and make our way to our cabana. I turn my back to him. He unbuttons the only button holding the back together. Once I move my hands, the dress slides down my body, leaving me standing there in the bodysuit and garter.

"I'm the luckiest man in the world. I get to undress you the rest of our lives."

Matt places kisses across my bare shoulders and neck. "I was standing in front of everyone with a hard-on when you walked out with that dress on. Thank gawd my shirt was long enough to cover me."

I turn to face him, kissing him deeply as I slowly unbutton his shirt, pushing it off his muscular shoulders, and down his arms. It falls to the floor next to my dress. I untie his linen pants, running my hands inside them along his waist slowly pushing them down.

I lead him backward toward the bed. When his legs bump into it, I urge him to sit down. I take his jockey shorts off as he raises his hips aiding me in sliding them off.

Wasting no time, I take Matt's hard cock into my mouth, gently scraping my teeth along his shaft as I back out. Then swallow him deeply over and over again. I cup his heavy balls in the palm of my hand, gently rolling them. Matt fists my hair, taking control of the speed as he fucks my mouth. I suck him deep, fighting the urge to gag as he jerks shooting his hot semen down my throat.

Matt falls back onto the bed. "Damn, Sable, you sucked my balls out of my dick."

"I'm sorry, I guess I'll never do that again." I pretend to pout and stand turning to walk away.

Matt grabs me around the waist and spins me, quickly pinning me on the bed. "You knew saying something like that was going to get you spanked, didn't you?"

"Maybe." I look over my shoulder at him with a grin.

Matt jerks the body suit off me, tossing it on the floor. He turns me on my side, pulls my arms behind my back, and cinches my wrists together with something that feels like hard plastic. My legs are quickly bent and my ankles are bound together as well. I look down and realize he has used zip ties.

"How did you get those?" I ask him, impressed. "Ms. Sally left us a gift basket. Gawd, I love that woman."

"She does seem to think of everything."

"You have no idea." I feel the bite of a paddle. Matt is holding a kid's paddle ball game with the ball and string missing.

I start laughing when I see the toy.

Matt gives me three more quick smacks. I can't help the moan that escapes. "I'm now a fan of paddle ball," I whisper.

"That's my girl." Matt gives me three more smacks.

"I'm so close," I cry out.

Matt buries his cock deep inside of me with one swift push, sending me over the edge. The more he pounds, the more the waves of my orgasm hit. Matt comes with his hand wrapped in my hair close to my scalp.

He cuts the zip ties and rubs my wrist and ankles with lotion after we take a nice warm shower together.

We lie in bed; I'm snuggled into Matt's side. "Matt, I love you."

"I love you too."

"Uhmm..."

"Sable, what is it?"

"I love Hawaii, but..."

"You're ready to go start our lives in our new home," Matt answers.

"Yes, you're not mad, are you?"

"No way, I want to see our playroom," he says like an excited kid.

I lift up to look at him. "Me too."

"Let's get some sleep and we will catch the first flight out tomorrow."

We arrive back in Los Angeles the next evening. We drive up into Hollywood Hills, stopping in front of our new home. It's the first time we have gotten to see it lit up at night with all the landscaping complete.

"Oh, Matt, it's beautiful."

"This is where we are going to raise our family."

We pull into the garage. Matt comes around to my door and opens it. I step out of the car, He swoops me up into his arms. "What are you doing?" I laugh.

"I'm carrying my bride across the threshold to our new home."

Once inside he sits me down. I look at him and grin before taking off toward the stairs. I'm going to be the first one to see the playroom. Matt catches me as I reach the top of the stairs. He carries me the rest of the way down the hall over his shoulder. He stops at the end of the hall laughing and puts me down to point at the door ahead of us. There was a sign on the door.

Welcome Home.
We knew you couldn't wait!

"Damn, we are that predictable." Matt laughs.

"Yes, and I wouldn't change it for anything. I love you, Mr. Jones."

"I love you, Ms. Jones." He unlocks the playroom. "Now strip."

"Yes, sir."

hate the sin...

LOVE THE SINNER.

Falling for the bad boys may get these ladies into trouble, but it's hard to resist the temptation. The guys are hot, talented, desperately wanted, famous... and the details of their stories extremely addicting.

As the women these athletes love peel away the layers, each one uncovers a side the public doesn't normally get to see. Whether or not that side is worth the fight is a different question.

One only answered by the heart.

7 Deadly Sins meet the famous athletes of the Players and Sinners Club. Indulge with these stand-alone stories, guilt-free.

Brought to you by:

KRISTY GIBS - Vanity Rush

CAM JOHNS- Ravenous Rebound

NANCY CHASTAIN- Craving Submission

M.K. MOORE - Gentleman's Anger

LAINE WATSON- Ruthless Keeper

LEXI NOIR- Jealous Stryker

SONYA JESUS- Pucking Nothing

about the author

Nancy's a wild child trapped inside a responsible adult. She found a release for my fun-loving disobedient self in writing. She loves tequila, dragons, and wizards. She has a collection of the mythical creatures that decorate her office. She finally allowed herself the time to go after her dream of writing. Her characters are stubborn, strong, full of emotion and cuss like sailors. (Just like her.)

Nancy has always had an interest in paranormal. Reading anything and everything she can on the subject of psychics and mediums. The theory that the average human only uses ten percent of their brain has always led her to wonder: What's a person capable of if they tapped into the other ninety percent?

She enjoys meeting new people and spending time with them discussing books. If you see her online or in person, be sure and say hello.

also by nancy chastain

Deadly Obsessions Series

- Obsession Book #1
- Betrayal Book #2
- Sacrifice Book #3 coming soon

The Caged Duet

- Caged Fear
- Caged Rage

Fairytale Retellings

- Beast

Other Novels

- Find Me
- Saving Charly

Made in the USA
Middletown, DE
04 April 2023

27771369R00130